The ma… r corner of the pool … get out … g in th… .

"Ian, … wate…

"You … a few s… allow…

Was this really happening? Was Ian kissing her? His lips felt so good that she couldn't help but put her arms around him and pull him closer. She opened her mouth and hungrily kissed him until she imagined herself purring with pleasure. "Mmm," she said with her eyes closed as the kiss ended.

Leaning into her, Ian kissed her eyelids, her forehead, her cheeks. He placed another soft kiss on her mouth and then said in a husky voice, "I wish I had known that all I had to do to shut you up was to kiss you."

Surry's eyes popped open. She pushed him away and jumped out of the pool. "I'm going to get dressed for dinner."

"Don't go. I was just beginning to enjoy myself," Ian called after her.

With hands on her hips, she turned back to face him. "You were enjoying yourself a bit too much. And I'd appreciate it if you don't let it happen again." With that she swung around and left the pool area with as much dignity as she could muster.

Books by Vanessa Miller

Kimani Romance

Her Good Thing
Better for Us
The Best of All

VANESSA MILLER

is a bestselling author, playwright and motivational speaker. She started writing as a child, spending countless hours either reading or writing poetry, short stories, stage plays and novels. Vanessa's creative endeavors took on new meaning in 1994 when she became a Christian. Since then, her writing has been centered on themes of redemption, often focusing on characters facing multidimensional struggles.

Vanessa's novels have garnered rave reviews, with several appearing on *Essence* magazine's bestseller list. Miller's work has received numerous awards, including a Best Christian Fiction Mahogany Award and a Red Rose Award for Excellence in Christian Fiction. Miller graduated from Capital University with a degree in organizational communication. She is an ordained minister in her church, explaining, "God has called me to minister to readers and to help them rediscover their place with the Lord."

The Best of All concludes Vanessa's For Your Love trilogy for Harlequin Kimani Romance.

VANESSA MILLER

HARLEQUIN® KIMANI™ ROMANCE

To Diamond—the best is truly yet to come for you. Believe it and receive all that God has for you.... All my love!

ISBN-13: 978-0-373-86323-5

THE BEST OF ALL

For questions and comments about the quality of this book, please contact us at CustomerService@Harlequin.com.

HARLEQUIN®
www.Harlequin.com

Printed in U.S.A.

Dear Reader,

Writing about Surry McDaniel and Ian Duncan was more like visiting two old friends. They were so easygoing that it felt as if I had known them for a lifetime but only now decided to write their love story.

You've read about Danetta and Ryla in the first two books of the For Your Love trilogy. Now I'd like to open the door to Surry's world in the final book of the series…and I guarantee you that it is definitely *The Best of All!*

Ian Duncan is not a man to be taken lightly. He's successful but dreams of even bigger success with the woman he has fallen in love with. Surry, on the other hand, has no time for love. She is on the fast track to success and isn't willing to stop for anyone…but Ian Duncan just might change her mind.

Thanks for taking the time to read *The Best of All.* I truly hope you enjoy reading this story as much as I enjoyed writing about Surry and Ian.

Happy reading,

Vanessa Miller

Chapter 1

"I love what you've done with this boutique. It is simply divine."

"Thanks, Ryla," Surry McDaniel told her friend, sweeping her gaze around the newly renovated boutique. "A lot of blood, sweat and tears went into the creation of Designs from the Motherland, so I'm glad that you think I made the right decision."

"Made the right decision? Are you kidding?" Ryla Carter took a silky white nightgown off the rack and held it up against her body. "If you had opened this store just three months ago, I would have worn this lovely number on my wedding night. I guarantee that Noel wouldn't have been able to resist me in this gown."

Surry joined their friend Danetta Windham in a chuckle. The three of them knew all too well that Ryla had tricked Noel into marrying her, and because of that the first night of the honeymoon was a complete disaster. It was good that they could finally laugh about it now.

"All's well that ends well," Danetta said.

"Yeah, but that hot mess didn't look like it was going to end so well," Surry reminded the group.

"Oh, but it did." Ryla strutted over to the checkout counter and laid the gorgeous nightgown on it. "And that is why I can still afford to purchase this expensive gown. Because my *husband*—" she lingered on the word *husband* for a long moment as she pulled out her black AmEx card "—can afford to keep me in the finest silks money can buy."

"Glad to hear it, because I use only high-quality material. My boutique is called Designs from the Motherland because everything comes from Africa. The fabric is light and airy, meant for weather like ours here in Houston Hotter-Than-Hades, Texas."

"Well, I'm going to purchase this fabulous swing skirt," Danetta announced as she held up a print skirt with vibrant blues and tans.

"I love that skirt," Surry said. "Everyone went wild for it last week."

"Oh, that's right. You had your first fashion show in Ghana. Tell us about it," Ryla said.

The three women poured themselves a cup of coffee and then retreated to the lounge area Surry had set up at the back of the boutique, which offered customers the luxury of relaxing and enjoying refreshments while being waited on by the staff. Designs from the Motherland wasn't an ordinary boutique. It was an experience.

Years ago she traveled across Africa, writing books about the culture and atmosphere in countries such as Kenya, Ethiopia, Zambia, Ghana and even Egypt, which tends to be commonly associated with the Middle East. She'd had the time of her life exploring and surrounding herself with people she could deeply identify with. Oh, she loved America and wouldn't trade her country for anything, but a piece of her heart was in the motherland.

However, her publishers didn't have the same love for the motherland as she did. And when the profits from her work failed to meet expectations, her line of coffee-table books was dropped. Since she was a child, her father was convinced that she would follow in his footsteps and be forced to live a meager existence, but Surry had other plans for her life.

Her mother had been a seamstress, working for little to no money, before arthritis set in and forced her to give it up. At the onset of the crippling disease, Surry stepped in and helped her mother finish orders that had been paid for previously. That was how Surry discovered that she had her mother's gift and began designing her own brand of African garb. The name Designs from the Motherland was twofold: acknowledging Africa and Surry's own mother. Surry had been determined to make a go of this business venture, and after seven years of struggling, she'd finally made it.

Her designs were now in hundreds of boutiques across the South and the East Coast thanks to her new distributor. In addition to the store she owned and operated in Houston, two chain retail stores were interested in carrying her line. Things were going so well for her that Surry should have expected something unexpected would turn her world around. But she never even saw her whirlwind coming.

"So tell us all about the fashion week in Ghana," Ryla said as the three women settled around the table.

"Girl, it was a blast. So many designers were there. I got my networking on, did my thing when it was time for my models to go on and then I kicked back and enjoyed the rest of the shows." She hesitated and then added, "That is, until the last day."

Danetta put her coffee mug down. "What happened?"

"Remember John Michael?"

"How could I forget him? The man had two first names and he smelled," Ryla said.

"That's not nice, Ryla. The man had a great love for garlic," Danetta said with a hint of humor in her tone.

"He also has a great love for lying."

Ryla, who'd been spreading vegetable cream cheese

on a wheat bagel, put the knife down and focused on Surry. "What has the stinky little man done?"

Sighing deeply, Surry shook her head in disbelief as she told her friends, "I think he must have fallen and bumped his head. Because he's running around telling anyone who will listen that I stole his designs. He even had the audacity to get in my face about it at the fashion show."

"You're kidding!" Danetta's mouth hung open.

"I wish I was. Last night a reporter called to ask me about his claims, so I guess I'll be seeing his lies in the newspaper pretty soon."

Danetta put her hand on Surry's shoulder. "That sounds awful."

"You haven't heard the worst of it yet." Surry covered her face with her hands and then dragged them down to her neck. "Things were going so well. Now I'm not sure how anything is going to turn out."

Her friends were silent, their attention centered on Surry.

"Remember the contracts I was supposed to be signing with Roukes?"

"Of course," Ryla said. "They're going to carry your designs in two of their chain department stores and make you a very rich woman."

Surry propped her elbows on the table and rested her chin in her hands. "That was the plan."

"What do you mean 'that was the plan'?" Danetta asked.

"One of the head buyers was in Ghana for fashion week. John Michael told her and everyone else his lies. My contract is on hold until I can straighten this mess out. And I've already spent all of my money increasing my production."

The group meditated on Surry's words for a moment, and then Danetta snapped her fingers and said, "You need one of those image consultants."

"No way." Surry shook her head. "People hire image consultants to fix problems they created for themselves, like Tiger Woods's girlfriends and that woman involved with that David Petraeus sex scandal. I haven't done anything wrong, and I don't want to make it seem like I need to fix a problem that I shouldn't even have."

"You didn't sleep with this guy, did you?" Ryla joked.

"Shut up, Ryla. You are so not funny." Surry was at her wits' end. She was about to lose everything she had worked so hard to build, and she had no idea how to make this train wreck go away. "Besides, I wouldn't even have the money to pay an image consultant if I had slept with him."

Ryla's eyes lit up. "I have the perfect person to help you, Surry."

"Did you just hear me say that I have no money? If I can't get that contract to go through, I don't know how I'm going to recoup the money I've spent on production."

"Girl, please." Ryla waved a hand in the air. "Ian Duncan would probably help you for free. You know he likes you."

"Ian Duncan is a campaign manager. How in the world could he help me with my problem? I'm not running for public office. I just want to sell my clothes."

"Ian is all about building the proper image. He helped Noel win his seat in Congress even after the reporters started hounding us about Noel being the father of a seven-year-old girl he knew nothing about."

She twisted her lip and ran her hands through her freshly straightened long black hair. Surry didn't believe in relaxers. They were accursed as far as she was concerned, manufactured only to strip the beauty and vitality from a woman's natural hair. But now the hot comb, that was a necessity. She knew that many felt the hot comb damaged the hair, as well. But as long as it was used sparingly, she didn't see a problem with it. "He asked me out, and I have yet to give him an answer."

"Well, now is as good a time as any to give the man an answer," Ryla said with a finger snap.

"I can't do that, Ryla. The man will think I'm awful…to only call on him when I'm in trouble and in need of his help."

"But you do need help, Surry. Maybe you need to drop your pride and call this guy," Danetta admonished.

"Look at it this way," Ryla tried. "Even if you're

not interested in dating Ian, he may still be able to help you. I'm not suggesting that you lead him on or anything like that. I just don't think you should pass up an opportunity to receive the help you need, simply because you're not interested in him."

Who said she wasn't interested in dating Ian Duncan? If the thought could even be imagined, the man was a much sexier version of the singer Eric Benet. Who wouldn't want to go out with him? It certainly wasn't that Surry didn't *want* to spend time with him. The problem was that she had neither the time nor inclination to get into a relationship. Her business, her success, came first, second and third. Her life had no room for a man, especially one like Ian Duncan.

"You both make good points. But you are forgetting that my mother gave me my name for one single reason...so that I would stand on my own and embrace my womanhood." Surry was short for Sojourner. She'd been named after the former slave turned abolitionist and women's rights activist. And she had fully embraced Sojourner Truth's famous "Ain't I a Woman" speech.

Ryla rolled her eyes at her friend. "We're well aware of this crazy man-hater mantra you live by."

Ryla and Danetta looked at each other and began reciting in unison the words from the speech Surry loved so much. "I have as much muscle as any man, and can do as much work as any man. I have plowed and reaped and husked and chopped and mowed, and can any man do more than that?"

"Hey," Surry interrupted, her feelings hurt. "My mother helped me memorize that speech word for word. And I have experienced a lot of success by the sweat of my own womanly hands."

"Yes, you have, Surry." Danetta was at her breaking point as she leaned toward her friend and said, "But now you need help, and there's no shame in that."

"Be a woman who is humble and wise enough to know when times have changed, and move with those changes."

"Okay, okay, you're right.... Maybe I do need to give Ian a call."

Ian Duncan was the hottest ticket in politics at the moment. He'd just finished a television interview with Anderson Cooper on CNN and then didn't even have time to change his shirt for the ten o'clock interview he had scheduled with Lawrence O'Donnell, the host of *The Last Word* on MSNBC. Tomorrow he would do it all over again with a few other hosts on radio and television. The recent presidential election had been a big deal, but after that the most pressing question on everyone's mind had been about the election of the reformed bad boy, Noel Carter.

Noel had been written off after news broke about his illegitimate child. Even Noel had thought he had a better chance of losing than winning. But Ian always believed in his client, and he'd devised a strategy that enabled Noel to hold a victory party on election night.

Done with his interviews for the evening, Ian threw off his suit and tie and jumped into the shower. As the hot water assaulted his body, Ian went over his next steps one by one. He had about a half dozen offers on the table from clients interested in working with him. At this point, Ian had to be very selective. He could take only those who fit into his eight-year plan.

Ian and Noel had been friends since college, so he'd taken the assignment knowing that if he lost, all the planning he'd done would be for naught. Congressional wins were nice, but Ian's eight-year plan included managing his first presidential campaign. So, from this point on, he wasn't taking on any more local campaigns. He was looking to run campaigns for senators and governors now. He just had to stay focused and work his plan.

As he stepped out of the shower and toweled off, Ian tried to turn his mind off work. A good night's rest was what he needed, but his thoughts quickly drifted to Surry McDaniel. He thought about giving her a call before he went to sleep. It had been two weeks since he asked her out, but he still hadn't received a response. The girl was definitely playing hard to get, but Ian had patience. From the moment he met Surry, Ian felt a connection. He had to find out more about this woman and he wasn't prepared to give up. Not just yet.

Dressed in a ribbed T-shirt and black silk pajamas, he threw back the covers and was about to get into bed when his phone rang.

He picked up the phone, and a nasally voice on the other end asked, "Is this Mr. Duncan?"

He sat down on the edge of his bed with the phone against his ear. "I know this is an old joke, but my father is Mr. Duncan. I'm simply Ian."

"Well, Ian, I have Governor David Monroe on the line. He would like to speak with you. Do you have a moment?"

Was this woman kidding? It was widely rumored that the popular North Carolina ex-governor was considering running for president. It was hard to believe, but the 2012 election had wrapped up only two weeks ago, and politicians were already putting out feelers for the next elections.

Ian certainly hadn't expected to hear from any presidential candidacy hopefuls—those political elites normally put in calls to his father. To date, Ian had handled mostly local, statewide and national congressional races. But he had every intention of becoming the kingmaker his father was several times over. "Of course I have time to speak with the governor. Please put him through."

"Ian, my boy, how've you been?" Governor Monroe greeted.

Ian had met the governor eleven years ago when he was interning for his father. Maybe the governor had reached out to him because he was trying to reconnect with the great Walker Duncan. "I've been wonderful, Governor. How have things been for you?"

"I've been working my backside off since I left the governor's mansion. And to tell you the truth, I'm itching to spend eight years in another mansion that just so happens to be in Washington, D.C."

"Are you sure you want to take that on? You've been a private citizen for two years now. Can't you think of anything more fun than running for president of the United States…like getting run over by a bulldozer and spending months in traction for instance?"

The governor laughed and then confessed, "I'm a political animal through and through. When it's in your bones, you can't quit even if you want to."

"So, what can I do for you, Governor?"

"I need a new campaign manager," Governor Monroe said without beating around the bush.

Ian wanted to leap, skip, jump and dance. This was it…his chance to prove to his father that he had what it took to be a kingmaker, just like him.

Governor Monroe was saying, "If you could come out to North Carolina so we can talk, then we could see if we will be a good fit for each other. How about it?"

"When would you like to meet?"

"Can you be here on Monday?"

Ian could be there tomorrow if need be. But he wasn't about to throw all his cards out just yet. "I'm still finalizing a few things from the last election. Can I give you a call back in the morning to see if I can get there by then?"

"That works, but I need to know something from you soon. I want to get a jump on this thing."

Ian hung up after promising to provide Governor Monroe with a final answer by midmorning of the next day. Ian went to sleep thinking that nothing could stop him from getting to Charlotte, North Carolina, by Friday.

By morning when he drove in to work and entered his office, he was gliding like a man who'd just been knighted. In Ian's wildest imagination he never would have thought that he'd get a chance to work on a presidential campaign this soon. Ian thought he'd have to continue proving himself through the Senate and gubernatorial elections. But now that this awesome opportunity has presented itself, Ian was going to ride it until the wheels fell off. Or better yet, he'd ride it all the way to a White House victory.

He rounded the corner, getting ready to greet his office manager, when out of the corner of his eye he spotted someone seated on the brown leather couch in the waiting area. Ian took a step back, peeked into the room and was caught off guard by the vision of loveliness before him.

He'd asked this woman out twice in the short time he'd known her. She'd never given him an answer, or even called him back for that matter. Ian had wracked his brain six ways from Sunday trying to figure out if he'd said or done anything to offend her. Maybe he'd drooled a bit too much when he was first introduced to her at Noel's wedding. But he couldn't help himself. She was an exotic beauty. Even this morning, with the way that white dress clung to her creamy cocoa-brown skin and her hazel eyes danced as she looked his way, he nearly stuttered as he said, "Surry, what are you doing here?"

Surry stood and sauntered over to him.

Ian wondered if Surry knew how seductive her movements were as she strutted toward him in a dress that accentuated her hourglass frame.

"I was hoping that you would be able to speak with me this morning. I need your help."

Her voice was as sultry as her image was exotic. She reminded him of one of those island beauties he'd seen on those "come to the beach" commercials, enticing folks to vacation in the Bahamas, Jamaica or some other place made for running barefoot in the sand. "Um, I think we should go to my office—" he pointed to the door across the hall "—so we can continue this conversation in private."

"Thanks. I appreciate that you would make time for me."

He'd like to do a lot more than make time for this woman. But so far, she hadn't been willing to give him the time of day. So, he was intrigued by this visit. Maybe he'd actually get that date before leaving for Charlotte.

Chapter 2

Things didn't seem so cut-and-dried anymore. Yes, Surry needed help, especially since some blogger interviewed John Michael and allowed the man to spill his lying guts to anyone with an internet connection. Her phone was ringing off the hook this morning with reporters asking her about John Michael's allegations. So, yeah, she needed help. But she didn't want to take advantage of Ian or get herself involved in something she couldn't easily get out of.

Crossing her legs to get comfortable on the sofa in Ian's office, she watched as he took his jacket off and slipped it around his high-backed chair. The man was a dream in motion. He was much lighter in complexion than any of the men she normally dated. The waviness of his hair also indicated to her that his parents were not of the same ethnic group. If she had to guess, she'd say one of his parents was white and the other black.

But none of that mattered to Surry. She was here in a strictly professional manner. She tried to turn her head away from the vision in front of her, because she truthfully couldn't care less that with his jacket off she could see that the man had biceps, triceps, muscular pecs and… *Watch yourself,* she admonished herself.

"Do you have some water? My mouth is a little dry," Surry said while scratching her throat and then coughing. It was getting hot in here. Surry felt like unbuttoning her top to get a little air, but decided against that.

"Sure." Ian opened the small fridge he kept in his office and pulled out an assortment of iced tea, Coke, root beer and a simple Pure Life water bottle. "Do you need anything else?"

"I'll just take the water."

Ian handed it to her, held back the iced tea for himself and then put the other bottles back in the fridge. "So, how's business at the new boutique?"

"How did you know I opened my boutique?" She hated the suspicious tone of her voice, but these days she didn't know whom she could trust. She prayed that Ian would be in her corner.

"Noel told me." He put down his drink and said,

"I haven't been checking up on you, if that's what you're worried about."

Shaking her head, Surry waved the notion away. "I'm sorry about the way I sounded just now. I guess I've just become a little paranoid during these past few weeks. I've got too much going on."

He sat down on the sofa next to her, giving her his full attention. "Want to tell me about it?"

"Where do I begin?" Surry was at her wits' end. The expansion deal for her clothing line was about to blow up in her face. No one would want to carry Designs from the Motherland if they thought she stole any of her designs. She'd be forever branded a fraud, and what customer in her right mind would want to wear the designs of a fraud?

"I know you're busy, so I don't want to waste your time by beating around the bush." Surry turned toward him and continued, "I was just about to sign a contract to have two very high-end chain retail stores carry my designs. In anticipation of this contract, I put all of my earnings into increasing production of my designs. Since John Michael started shooting his mouth off, the contract has been put on hold. And to tell you the truth, I don't know what I'm going to do."

"What kind of claims?"

"He says that the designs for my spring and summer collection were stolen from him."

"Did you and he work on designs together?"

"Never! I don't like John Michael's designs, but

we worked a few fashion shows together and split the cost of both rentals at two expos about seven years ago. But since then I haven't collaborated with him or anyone else. To tell you the truth, I much prefer to work on my own."

"A loner, huh?"

She didn't like the way he said "loner." He made it sound as if there was something wrong with a girl needing her space and preferring to work alone. But Surry saw nothing wrong with her choices. Besides her girls, Danetta and Ryla, Surry didn't hang out with anyone. She had a business to run and that required most, if not all of her time. But that didn't make her a *loner,* did it? She shrugged, "Okay, yeah, I like being alone. I do my best designs that way. No television, no music…just me and the chirping of the crickets."

"That must be how you creative types like to do your work. Me, I'd go crazy if I didn't have my iPod or my radio going most of the time. I love music and it helps me think."

"To each his own, I guess."

"Yeah, I guess so," Ian said, and then silence fell. After a few moments, he rubbed his hands together. "So, how can I help you?"

"Ryla says that you're a good guy and the best when it comes to handling image problems."

"Ryla said that, huh?" There was a slight smile on his face, as if he wanted to break out into a laugh from things he knew, but wouldn't say.

"She sure did. So, after John Michael did this blog interview—" she handed him the interview that she'd printed off the internet "—and then his lies got reported in the paper this morning, I rushed over here, hoping that you could help me. I've never had to deal with anything like this before. So I didn't know what else to do."

Was he hearing her right? She hadn't bothered to respond to his offer of dinner, and she was in his office at this moment only because she needed an image makeover? He stood, read the blog that she handed him and then turned back to her. "This guy obviously has a problem with the success you've had with your line of clothing. But I'm not sure how I can help you."

Flipping her hair off her shoulder, she said, "I don't know, either. I'm about to lose everything if John Michael gets away with the lies he's spreading. Ryla spoke so highly of the way you were able to help Noel, that I just..." Her shoulders slumped as her voice cracked. Her eyes said that she'd rather be anywhere but here, dealing with this issue. "I just hoped that you would be able to do something to help me also."

The woman he met at Noel and Ryla's wedding was dynamic, self-assured, ready to take on the world. But Surry looked so helpless as she sat on his couch worrying about losing everything that he wished he could help. But how on earth could he help her and work his own plan?

Ian Duncan was nothing if not focused. He knew from the day he first interned with his father that he would be in the game of politics for the rest of his life. Even with the craziness now going on in Washington, Ian still desired this life as he desired his next breath. Thankfully, he'd never wanted the frustrating job of being a politician. He wanted to be the puppet master, the one behind the scene pulling all the strings, making kings of mere men. His father had become known as a kingmaker because he'd headed three campaigns that had catapulted two former governors and one former statesman into the White House.

It was now Ian's turn to prove that he had what it took to be a kingmaker. Since his college days, Ian had vowed to let nothing stop him from achieving his goals. He'd loved playing basketball but had never been interested in going pro. He'd spent years giving all he had to the game of politics, and at the age of thirty-one he was about to reap the fruits of his labor. He couldn't allow this thing with Surry to get him off his game. He'd be a fool to help her when the prize he'd strived for all this time was now waiting for him in Charlotte.

Looking at Surry was not helping him. He wanted to scoop her up and protect her from the storm. But to do that, he'd have to put his own dreams on hold, and Ian couldn't do that. He averted his eyes. When that proved to not be enough, he went and stood in front of the window that overlooked the parking lot and then said, "I know politics. I don't know the first thing about fashion. So, I'm not sure that I'm the one to help with this issue."

Surry stood and walked over to the window. She put her hand on Ian's shoulder and turned him to face her. Her eyes implored him as she said, "You don't understand. If you don't help me I could lose everything. I've worked so hard for what I have. I can't lose it just because of a lie."

He rested a hand on her arm as he leaned against the windowpane. This woman was so beautiful. She was everything he wanted in his personal life. But he was also a professional. "Surry, believe me, it's not that I don't want to help you. I can't. I will be leaving the state in a few days to talk with a man who is interested in running for president. If he and I decide to work together, I'm going to be very busy trying to build a team to get his campaign up and running."

Running her hand through her hair, she looked at him with determination in her eyes. "The sad part about it is that I was prepared to come over here and beg for your help if I had to, and you wouldn't have been able to help me even if I had begged." She patted him on the shoulder, stepped back and said, "Congratulations on the new client. I'll find a way to resolve this issue."

As Ian watched Surry walk away, he wanted to reach out and pull her back to him. Was he a fool? How could he let her walk away like this? The phone on his desk started ringing, jarring his mind back to the business at hand. As she closed his office door, he picked up the phone. "Ian speaking."

"Well, my boy, what's it going to be?"

Ian wanted to tell Governor Monroe that he was no one's boy…had been his own man since he was nineteen and wasn't trying to go back to school for nobody. However, this man might become the next president of the United States of America, so he'd hold off on telling him how he could and couldn't address him. "Hey, Governor, I was just in a meeting. But if you hadn't called me, I would have given you a call within five minutes or so."

"I don't have the patience of Job, my boy. I'm a man of action. I gave you the night to think about it, so what's it going to be? Can I expect to see you in Charlotte on Monday or not?"

Ian went back to the window and watched Surry climb in her Mercedes C300. He didn't know why, but Ian felt in his gut that he would forever regret not being able to help Surry. But he had a business to run, so he closed his eyes and took the plunge. "One question, Governor. Why me?"

"What kind of fool question is that? I was told that you are the best and I want to work with you."

Ian had his answer and he was fine with it. "You can count on me, Governor. I'll be there on Monday."

"That's what I wanted to hear. I'm looking forward to going over strategy with you."

Surry was driving out of his life as he said, “Oh, and one more thing, Governor. You won’t ever have to doubt my loyalty to you. I live and breathe this job. So, I’m your man and we are going all the way to the White House.”

Chapter 3

On Saturday morning Ian went to the strip mall near his condo and purchased a few items for his upcoming trip. He then met Noel Carter at the Breakfast Klub for some waffles and wings. "Have you found a place to stay in Washington yet?" he asked his old friend.

Noel shook his head. "Ryla and I are going out there next week to look around."

"I'm headed out of town next week myself. I can't give you a name right now, but I'm meeting with someone who is thinking of running for president."

Joy spread across Noel's face. "That's all right. I'm excited about that. You go handle his campaign, and then in about a decade or so, you and I will be working on my presidential campaign."

"Now that sounds good to me. We will have another President Carter in the White House."

"Yeah, but I'm going to be there for two terms."

The men ate their food and then Noel put his fork down and said, "I'm not going to be able to go home if I don't ask you something."

"What's up?"

"Ryla wants to know if you talked with Surry."

"She came by my office yesterday. I feel for her, because this guy is trying to do a number on her. But I have to leave town on Monday morning, so I'm not sure I can help her." Ian didn't mention to Noel that he was also bothered by the fact that Surry couldn't pick up a phone to accept his dinner invitation. But the moment she needed help, she came right over to his office. But he wasn't bitter, so he was trying hard not to act like it.

After breakfast he went home and started packing for his trip to Charlotte, still trying to convince himself that he made the right decision. He was almost there, until he turned on the television and caught a glimpse of a tearful Surry on the six o'clock news. The reporter had obviously just asked her a question as he'd turned to this station. The microphone had been shoved in Surry's face. Maybe no one else noticed, but he took note of the tears on her eyelashes as she declared, "My business means everything to me. I would never jeopardize losing it by stealing from a former colleague."

Surry was going to be crucified in the media unless she did something to change the situation fast. She didn't deserve what was being done to her. And Ian knew firsthand that once the media got hold of something, they wouldn't let it go until they ruined the lives of everyone associated. He put a pair of pants in the suitcase and sat down on his bed, thinking about the pain he saw in Surry's eyes as she talked about how much her business meant to her. Where did pain like that come from? Then he wondered if he was wrong about what he thought he saw in her eyes...maybe it had been passion for her business. Pain or passion, he wasn't sure which, but he desperately wanted to find out.

Making a quick decision, Ian grabbed his keys and drove to Westheimer Road. He'd received an invitation to the grand opening of Designs from the Motherland from Ryla. Ian had been out of town handling some business in Washington so he hadn't been able to make the opening. But he'd kept the invitation and therefore had the address.

Her shop was exactly twenty-seven minutes away from his condo. He parked next to the cute little Mercedes he'd seen her drive off in the other day and stepped out of his Range Rover.

Walking toward her store, Ian noticed smiling customers walking from one shop to another with their purchases. The area was vibrant and active. This was a good spot for business. Ian was admiring Surry's business savvy as he watched her ring up a customer. At the front of the store he couldn't hear what the customer said to her, but he could see Surry lean her head back and give a full-throated laugh. He could spend a lifetime with a woman who laughed like that.

Surry handed the customer her bag, and as she walked away, Ian stepped over, put his hands on the counter and asked, "Why does it matter to you so much?"

"Why does what matter to me?"

He waved a hand around, indicating the building they were standing in. "Your business…I saw you on the news this evening, and I remembered the way you looked in my office the other day. This whole thing has hit you really hard, and I want to know why you're letting it get to you like this."

Averting her eyes, staring at the cash register rather than Ian, she said, "My business means a lot to me. I've worked hard to get where I am. And it just bugs me that someone can lie on me, and I can't even fight back."

"Of course you can fight back. Why do you think I'm here?"

"I don't know why you're here, because the last I heard, you have a plane to catch. So, just go away and let me figure out how to deal with John Michael on my own. I never should have bothered you in the first place."

"You are infuriating and stubborn, Surry McDaniel." He walked behind the counter and pulled her close to him. "You need to understand that I don't want to leave town without you." She was so close that he was inhaling the vanilla scent of her perfume. He didn't know why, but that sweet, welcoming fragrance made him want to put his face in the crook of her neck and sniff her like a lovesick pup.

"You have to leave," Surry was saying. "You have an important client and I can't stand in the way of that, no matter how dire my situation has become."

"I want you to go with me."

Surry stepped around Ian and sat down at the table in the back of her boutique. Ian followed her, and she said, "What are you thinking, Ian? I can't just pick up and leave town with you."

He pulled out a chair and sat down across from her. "Why not? Things aren't going so good for you here."

"I have a business to run, if you hadn't noticed." Surry stretched forth her hand, indicating the things that were in her boutique.

"You won't have much of a business to run if the media start crucifying you. We have a limited amount of time to turn this situation around. And I can't repair your image and provide damage control unless I spend some time figuring out who you really are and what makes you tick."

"And just like that—" she snapped her fingers "—my problems will be over."

"Well, not like that." He mimicked her finger snapping. "I also plan to find out as much about your rival as possible. If we can dig up enough dirt on him, we'll be able to change his tune pretty quick." Ian might not know fashion, but he knew mankind. And in politics, avoiding scandal was the name of the game. So, if this John Michael had skeletons, he planned to find them.

"Oh, it's 'we' now, is it?"

"Excuse me?" He was caught off guard by her attitude.

"When I came to you yesterday, you said you wouldn't be able to help me. Now you're sitting here making all these plans, even though you have a very important client to handle. So, I just want to know what gives. What's in it for you?"

This woman was so stubborn. Ian almost got up and walked back out the door. He had a life and really didn't need this right now. But the truth was, he knew that she needed him, whether she wanted to admit it or not. "I want to help you, Surry. But I'm scheduled to get on a plane first thing Monday morning. So, if you want the help, you'll have to travel with me so I can figure out how we'll fix this mess you've stepped in."

She leaned back in her chair and stared at him.

It felt as if those hazel eyes were seeing into his soul. Ian squirmed in his seat a bit. "What's with all the staring? Do I have food in my teeth or something?"

"I can't date you."

Ian looked around the room and then back at Surry. "Who asked you out?"

"You did—" she pointed at him "—you big goof. And now you're asking me to go out of town with you. I just don't want you getting the wrong impression."

"You don't have to worry about that anymore. I like my women a lot less obstinate than you are. I'm over you." He lifted his hand like a man standing before a judge and pledging to tell the truth, and then he winked.

"I'm serious, Ian. Men are always acting as if they understand my reasons for not wanting a relationship, but everything changes after a few dates."

He put his elbows on the table and leaned in. "So, men just can't resist you, huh?"

"That's not what I said." She lifted a finger and then continued. "Men don't like the word *no,* and they will chase after any woman who's not chasing after them."

Ian chuckled. "Is that right?"

"You know I'm right."

Ian stood and pulled the keys out of his pocket. "Well, the offer stands. We can even get separate rooms." He started walking away and then turned back and added, "Let me know by tomorrow and I'll book you on the flight with me."

After church, Surry, Danetta and Ryla went to a café for brunch. Surry ordered the fresh fruit platter with low-fat yogurt and a small coffee cake.

Danetta smiled at the server as she said, "I'll take the full breakfast."

Ryla licked her lips and set her menu down. "That sounds fab. I'll have what Danetta's having."

Surry gave her friends a curious look. The three of them always got the fruit platter with yogurt for breakfast, unless one of them had a taste for a waffle with strawberries. But on no occasion had any of them decided to inhale eggs, bacon, hash browns, pancakes and fruit. Danetta used to eat a whole pan of brownies and a gallon of ice cream whenever Marshall started dating a new woman. But those days were over. She and Marshall were now married. Surry handed her menu to the server and asked her friends, "What gives? Why are you two ordering enough food to feed a family of five?"

"I just seem to be extra hungry these days," Danetta said with a devious grin.

Ryla lightly punched Danetta's arm. "Stop playing. Let's tell her."

With an eyebrow lifted, Surry asked, "Are my two best friends…or shall I say, my two *only* friends, keeping secrets from me?"

"No, girl. We just found out yesterday."

Surry gave them a look that said "spill it."

"Well, Ryla went to the doctor yesterday," Danetta began.

"And when I told Danetta what the doctor said, she said she just had this weird feeling that something was up with her also. So she purchased a test, and wouldn't you know, she passed it."

"What are you two talking about?" Surry demanded.

"We're pregnant," the two said in unison.

She should have known this day would come, but honestly, Surry was shocked.

"Well, say something, girl," Ryla demanded.

The waitress brought their drinks to the table and set a glass of orange juice in front of Surry and Danetta and then handed Ryla a glass of apple juice. Surry lifted her orange juice and toasted her friends. "Congratulations to both of you. Noel and Marshall must be over the moon."

"They're excited, all right. Marshall already went out and bought cigars." Danetta laughed.

"And having the kids at the same time is going to be wonderful, because they will be able to do play dates together," Surry said.

"We just need one more baby for the play date to be complete," Danetta said with a pointed stare at Surry.

Shaking her hands vigorously, Surry said, "Don't look at me. I don't have time for a man or a baby. But I'll tell you what Aunty Surry can do. I'll design them some baby clothes."

"Oh, Surry, that's awesome! I'm picturing a whole new line of sleek and stylish Designs from the Motherland for babies."

Surry held up a hand. "Hold on there, Ryla. I was

just talking about a few outfits for Danetta's and your babies. I have way too much on my plate to work on a kids' line. If this new contract goes through, I will be working night and day finalizing everything."

"Why are you even allowing *if* in your mouth? That is such a negative and faithless word. You need to take back your power on that one," Danetta said.

"Everybody can't walk on water, Danetta. Some of us normal human beings sink when we try that stuff." In the past year, Danetta had been such a powerhouse of faith that she didn't doubt God on anything. Surry was having a little more trouble. Her business was all she had, and if she lost it, she had nothing. She'd be just another loser added to the long line of losers in the McDaniel family.

"Did you call Ian like I suggested?" Ryla asked as she accepted her platter of eggs, bacon and hash browns from the waitress. The waitress then set a smaller plate of pancakes and a bowl of grits in front of Ryla.

Surry picked up her fork as her platter of fruit and low-fat yogurt was set in front of her. "Yes, I contacted Ian. I even went to his office and spoke with him face-to-face."

Danetta received her food.

"What did he say?" Ryla pressed. "Can he help you?"

She hesitated and then said, "He would like to help me, but he has to be out of town for the next week or so, and then he's going to be bogged down with the work he'll have to do for his new client."

Talking between bites, Ryla said, "But he told you he'd make time for you, right?"

"Yeah, if I decide to go out of town with him. But I don't think that's a good idea." Surry bit into her pineapples and watermelon, loving the refreshing taste of the fruit. She looked over and watched as her friends gorged on carbs and fat. It was almost too much for her to watch. She pointed at their plates. "If you keep eating like this, you'll be too big to fit in the delivery room."

"Hush up, Surry. Just let me enjoy this for a week or two." Ryla inhaled more of her food and then added, "How many times in life does God bless us with excuses to eat like pigs? And anyway, you're just trying to change the subject."

"Yeah," Danetta agreed, using her fork to point in Surry's direction. "You're attracted to Ian. That's why you don't want to go out of town with him."

"Oh, please," Surry scoffed. "Ian is the one with the attraction problem. But I have told him that I have no time in my life for a relationship."

"Why don't you make time, Surry? What is so wrong with sharing your life with a man who makes you happy?" Ryla asked.

"Marriage and kids is something the two of you wanted. But I'm not wired that way. I would sooner curl up with my pillow and the knowledge that my business is a success than waste time cultivating some relationship that's doomed to fail from day one anyway."

Shaking a finger at her, Danetta admonished, "Oh ye of little faith. How can you just count yourself out like that?"

"Or—" Ryla squinted as she stared at Surry "—maybe Surry is so attracted to Ian—I mean, who wouldn't be, the man is gorgeous—that she can't stand to be alone with him. She'd even risk losing the business she claims to love so much if it means that she has to be in the same room with Ian."

"That's not fair, Ryla. I would do anything to save my business. I'm just not so sure about Ian's motives is all."

"What do you care about his motives? If he makes a move, just tell him that you're not interested and then accept all the help he can give you. This is about your business." Ryla knocked on the table and then used her knuckles to place a few light taps on Surry's head. "You know, the one that's in trouble at the moment."

"Bad press can do irreparable damage to a business, Surry. You don't want this thing to linger," Danetta said.

Ryla was right and so was Danetta. It was time for action. All Surry had ever wanted was her business, and now that it was being threatened, she needed to do whatever was necessary to save it. After all, if her business failed, there would be nothing else for her to fall back on. She wasn't like her friends. She didn't have a husband and children to look forward to.

All Surry had ever planned for was to be a success. She only hoped that in years to come, she wouldn't look back and wonder if she'd made the right decision.

Chapter 4

Surry called one of her staff members the moment she got into the car heading home. She wanted to check and see if her assistant manager would be able to cover her at the boutique for a week. When Brenda Ann answered the phone, she said, "Hey, I just wanted to check in and see how things are going at the boutique."

"Things are going really well. The customers are happy with the selections we have on the floor. And Sherry showed up on time for her shift, so I'm good."

"I think you're on the schedule every day this week, right?"

"Yep, sure am."

"I might have to leave town for a few days. Do you think you can handle the boutique on your own?"

"Child, I've been working in retail for thirty years. If I can't handle a few days on my own, I need to throw in the towel."

Surry laughed. "Okay, Brenda Ann. I appreciate your willingness to help out. I'll see you in a few days."

"I'll call and give you a report every evening."

"That will work. Thanks."

Once she had someone to stand in for her, she called Ian.

When he picked up the phone, she said, "I'll go."

"Well, hello, Ms. Surry McDaniel. I'm doing well. How are things going with you?"

She smiled. Ian was crazy. "Okay, sorry about that. I obviously wasn't raised right."

"Don't blame your parents for your bad manners," Ian said good-naturedly.

Surry was in no mood to discuss her parents, so she simply asked, "How are you, Ian?"

"Doing good. Just finished packing and I was getting ready to fix myself a steak for dinner."

"I just finished having brunch with Danetta and Ryla."

"Oh, really? Did Ryla tell you the good news?"

Surry wasn't sure how she felt about Ian knowing Ryla's good news before she did. But Noel and Ian were friends, so she could understand that Noel would want to tell someone about the baby. "I got a double dose of good news today. Not only is Ryla pregnant, but our friend Danetta found out that she is pregnant, as well. I couldn't believe it. But they are very happy."

"What does that make you, an auntie or a godmother?"

Surry thought about her friends for a moment and instantly knew how it would play out. She said, "Ryla will most likely make Danetta her baby's godmother and I'll become the godmother to Danetta's baby."

"So does that mean Ryla is out of the godmother business until you settle down and have a baby?"

"Don't you start that crazy talk, too. How many times do I have to say that I am happy with my career and don't need anything else to fulfill me. I'm a woman with a plan that does not include a man and a bunch of babies."

"If you say so," Ian said in a disinterested voice. "Let me get off the phone so I can book your flight and I'll give you a call back with the details."

"No!" Surry yelled.

"No, what?"

"I don't want you paying for my ticket, or my hotel room for that matter. So, just give me the flight number and I'll book my own flight."

Ian chuckled.

"Why do you keep laughing at me?"

"I'm not laughing at you. I just find it funny that you need help, but refuse every attempt I make to offer it." He sighed deeply and then added, "You can pay me back if you want to, but I need to book the flight, because I want to sit next to you so we can talk while we're in the air."

She didn't like his crack about her refusing the help she so obviously needed, but she allowed Ian to win the argument, or better yet, the discussion. He ordered the tickets while she went home to pack.

The next morning Surry threw on a paisley-print caftan with a V-neck and V-shaped hemline. The knee-length dress had gold and purple swirls, and Surry felt like an African princess with it on. It was also comfortable, and since she was going to be in and out of airports today, she was opting for comfort. A little sex appeal didn't hurt, either. Sometimes it got a woman through the lines faster.

Surry caught a cab to the airport and got out in front of the terminal where her nonstop flight to Charlotte would be taking off. She gave the cab driver a tip after he took her bags out of the trunk. She looped her tote bag over the handle of her suitcase. She then grabbed hold of the handle and easily carted her belongings into the airport without the help of any man. All she needed was the trusty wheels on the bottom of her suitcase. Move out of the way, men. She was woman and could handle her own business.

She stood just inside the airport. Her head swung back and forth as she looked for Ian. She heard someone holler her name. But it didn't sound like Ian, so she kept looking.

"Surry," the man said again as he grabbed her arm and turned her to face him.

She plastered a smile on her face as she turned and greeted Greg Thompson. She'd gone out with him a few times last year because she thought he was a player who wasn't looking for a serious relationship. Boy, was she wrong. "Hey, Greg, how've you been doing?"

"Not so good. I've been waiting on a certain lady to return my call." He looked at his watch and then back at her. "For about a year now."

She hated confrontations like this. But Surry also thought that it was always best to be up-front and honest, so she took a deep breath and said, "I'm really too busy to get involved in a serious relationship."

"Who's asking for serious?" Greg gave her a nudge. "I was just thinking we could hang out…you know, like we used to."

"How's that new business of yours going? What was it?" She snapped her fingers. "Sporting goods?"

"Actually, I did sporting goods when we first met. The last time we spoke I had opened a shoe business, but it didn't go so well." He started making hand gestures, as if he was conducting a workshop and explaining some things to the group. "Look, I understand how it is with you now. You want your freedom—no rules, no labels. I can flow with that. Just give me a call."

She put her arm on his shoulder, still giving him

that I-pity-you look. “Greg, listen, you are a really nice guy, but—”

“Honey.” Ian kissed Surry on the forehead and put his arm around her waist. “We’re going to miss our flight if we don’t get going.”

Surry looked up at Ian. He was her knight in shining armor coming to her rescue, and at that moment she wanted to thank him by wrapping her arms around him and planting a lingering kiss on his perfectly luscious lips. But since she didn’t want to start anything that she couldn’t finish, she came to her senses quickly. “Hey, I’ve been looking for you.”

“Is that right?” Ian asked as he turned his attention to Greg.

“Who is this?” Greg asked Surry, with possession clinging to his tone.

Ian stuck his hand out. “Ian Duncan.”

Greg shook Ian’s hand as he introduced himself. “Greg Thompson.”

“Well, come on. We don’t want to miss our flight,” Ian told Surry as he put his hand around the handle of her suitcase.

“I got it,” Surry said, pulling back from him.

“I don’t mind,” Ian told her as he took the suitcase and began walking toward the check-in desk.

Surry would have protested the taking of her suitcase as if she was some helpless female who couldn’t walk a few steps without begging for the help of some big, strong man. But Greg was watching them, and

Ian had done a good job of convincing him that they were a couple. She wasn't about to do anything to take that image out of Greg's mind. "Well, see you another time." She waved at Greg as she rushed to catch up with Ian.

When she found him, he had pulled their tickets from the kiosk and was getting ready to wrap a tag around the handle of her suitcase. "I can do it," Surry told him as she took the tag away from him.

After completing the task, she glanced over at Ian and noted that he was laughing at her again. She refused to say anything to him about it this time. If he wanted to spend his life being a laughing hyena, then who was she to stop him?

He pointed at the tag. "You took it from me before I could tell you to write your name on it." He handed her an ink pen.

"Good thinking. If they lose the suitcase, they'll know where to send it if my name and address are on the tag." She bent down and wrote her information on the tag, knowing that he was laughing at her again. She couldn't take the embarrassment one more minute, so when she stood she said, "Okay, I like to do things myself. Is that such a crime? I am, after all, single and have learned to do things myself."

Ian pointed in the direction where they'd just seen her friend. "Greg what's-his-name would love to do any and everything you ask. The man looked positively lovestruck when I arrived."

She took her tote off the suitcase and handed the luggage to the steward. "Just a case of a man not being able to take no for an answer."

"Is that right?" Ian asked as he also handed over his bag and then began walking to the security checkpoint.

"Sure is." Surry took her shoes off and went through the security area. After leaving security and heading for their plane, Surry added, "Look, I have no illusions about men chasing after me because I'm the most beautiful, intelligent or witty woman on earth." She lifted her hands and twirled around. "Goddess material, I'm not."

"So you say," Ian answered while staring at her with a hunger he couldn't suppress.

Shaking her finger at him, she said, "The way I see it is like this—men chase after me because I don't want to commit myself to them. I'm more of a free spirit and fully concentrating on making a success of my business."

"And you can't have a successful business and a man?" Ian inquired.

Surry shook her head. "One would be a distraction from the other."

"Now see, that just goes to show how much I know. Because I'd always thought that having success in business and in love would be the best of both worlds."

What Ian considered the best of both worlds, Surry considered a distraction that she didn't need. Lately, she'd given up the idea of even hanging out with a man and dating with no strings attached. She had a business to run and wasn't about to let anyone tie her down before it was in the black.

But Surry could admit that seeing her two best friends so happy about their pregnancies yesterday did something to her. She went home last night and, as she lay in bed all alone, wondered if she had made the right decision with her life. But one single thing kept Surry on her path. That was the memory of how all of her father's failures affected his family.

A man who can't take care of his family shouldn't have one. And with Surry's business in shambles, she couldn't even consider finding someone to marry and have a child with. Her friends had chosen their paths in life, and she had chosen hers. Simple as that.

"What are you thinking about?" Ian asked after they had boarded the plane and were seated next to each other waiting for takeoff.

"What…huh? Oh, nothing."

"It didn't look like nothing. Your eyes were like this." He put his face in front of hers and scrunched his eyelids 'til she could barely see his pupils. "So, I know you were thinking about something pretty serious. 'Fess up, Surry. If you were thinking about me, just admit it."

She laid her head on the headrest and turned to Ian. "Are you just being nosy, or do you really want to know my thoughts?"

"It seemed like you were thinking about something important, but if it was too personal, I don't want to pry."

Now it was Surry's turn to chuckle it up. The man was out of control. "I thought that was what this trip was all about…me giving you time so you can get all up in my business."

Ian raised a hand. "I'm not trying to be nosy. I need to know a lot more about you than I currently know if I'm going to figure out how to help you."

"This image-building stuff is hard work, huh?" Surry's eyes lit up as she smiled at Ian. She didn't know when it occurred, but she felt comfortable with him. Comfortable enough to let loose and talk to him. "Okay, so what do you want to know about me?"

Chapter 5

Everything and then some was what he wanted to know about the elusive Ms. Surry McDaniel, who claimed not to be a goddess but in his book was pretty doggone close. He tapped his chin with a fingertip. "Let's see. What do I want to know?" He turned toward her and then let his eyes slowly trail the length of her body, stopping at her shapely legs. The dress she had on was knee-length, but when she sat down, as she was now, it exposed her muscular thighs. "Are you a runner?"

Surry looked down and spotted where his eyes had traveled. "I prefer to use the EFX machine and to do a bit of fast walking. Running is bad on the knees."

After saying that, she held out her hand. "Can I borrow your jacket, please?"

He took the jacket off and placed it across her lap. And then with a smirk, he said, "If you don't want anyone to see your legs, you may need to start wearing full-length dresses."

"Or maybe old men should stop leering at me," she suggested as she positioned his coat jacket so that it covered her thighs and the tops of her legs.

"Woman, you wound me." Ian touched his heart as if it were breaking. "Calling me an old man is like saying I'm just like my father."

"Don't most men want to be like their father?"

"Not this man," Ian said and then turned the tables on her. "But we're not here to talk about me. Tell me, Surry, did you design the dress you have on?"

Surry looked down at her dress, enjoying the gold-and-purple color of it. She nodded. "I found the fabric in West Africa. I love the feel of it and thought other women would also, so to answer your question, yes, I did make this dress."

"So why African apparel?" Ian put his elbow on the armrest as he put his hand under his chin and leaned in while they talked. It was true that he needed to know more about her so he could build the image they would present to the media, but Ian was fascinated by Surry.

"I just love the look and feel of the material. Since

my first trip to Africa, I've been purchasing outfits from them."

"Were you purchasing the clothes so that you could work on your own designs? Was that your original purpose for going to Africa?"

"Not at all," Surry said. "I used to be a travel writer. I chose to write about places like Ghana, Kenya, Haiti and a few other places in Africa. When the books stopped selling and my travel writing career was over, I decided the best thing for me to do would be designing clothes that I love."

"How did you feel when you discovered you wouldn't be able to write anymore?" Ian asked.

"I understood the decision, so I wasn't bitter. But I knew I had to figure out a new life for myself. So I didn't have time to wallow over a career that was ending. I had to figure out what my new life was going to look like."

Surry had managed to impress Ian without even trying. Most people would have wallowed in self-pity after losing a career they loved, but not Surry. She just dusted herself right off and went out and made another life for herself. "Wow. That's awesome. I don't know what I could do if I couldn't be involved in politics."

"But you're not a politician," Surry reminded him.

Shaking his head, Ian told her, "I've never ever wanted to be an actual politician. I get more of a thrill out of the making of politicians."

"So you're the kingmaker, huh?"

"Up to this point, I've only been the duke and princemaker. But if things go the way I want them to go in Charlotte, then yeah, you could call me a kingmaker."

She pointed at his eyes. "Your face lit up as you talked about becoming a kingmaker. So I would say that you've definitely picked the right career for yourself."

Smiling, Ian said, "Judging by the outfits I've seen you in, I'd say you picked the right career also."

"My mother was a seamstress, so I guess it came naturally to me."

They continued to talk about Surry and her adventures until they reached the subject of Haiti. Surry told Ian that she gave ten percent of her profits to the rebuilding of schools in Haiti. Ian then confessed that he'd gone to Haiti in 2010 to help with the cleanup after that awful storm.

"Shut up!" Surry said, becoming more animated with the movements of her arms. Even though they had their seat belts on because they were, after all, flying high in the sky, Surry couldn't help but turn her body even more toward him. "You went to Haiti?"

Ian nodded. "Sure did. I got there in February. I was working with four clients for the elections at the time. Things were going poorly from the start. I needed to regroup in order to rethink my strategy, and the people of Haiti needed some houses built."

"How did it go?"

"About a million Haitians had lost their homes. So the group I went down there with spent two weeks cleaning up rubble and rebuilding as many homes as we could."

"You know that your eyes lit up again," Surry told him. But this time, instead of just pointing at his eyes, she leaned over and touched his cheek just under one eye. "Maybe you need to reevaluate your career also."

Ian shook his head. "I'm in the right place. I'm not a complicated man. I am a product of my birth. My father is a political animal, and my mom is a giver. She believes that people should give money, time or both if it is a worthy cause." He shrugged his shoulders and added. "So, politics and giving to others excites me."

"Are those the only two things that excite you?" Surry teased.

"Looking at your legs excited me, but you covered those up."

She shoved him. "Shut up, Ian. And anyway, when I asked how it went, I wasn't asking about Haiti. I know how things are going there. I wanted to know about the elections you had so much trouble with in 2010."

"Oh." Ian was surprised by the way the conversation had turned. He didn't spend much time talking about himself. Usually, he was talking up his client or finding out things about his client to talk about. "Okay, well, by the time I left Haiti my head was clear, and I got back into the States and won three out of the four campaigns we'd been working on. Number four still blames my trip to Haiti for his loss."

Surry laughed. "I bet he never had a chance in the first place."

Ian turned serious as he looked her in the eye and said, "I've never taken on a client that I didn't believe in. And that includes you, Surry McDaniel."

Her eyes moistened as she laid her hand on his arm. "You really believe that I have a chance to turn this thing around?"

"I wouldn't have invited you on the trip if I didn't."

"Thanks for saying that, Ian." Their eyes met and held a moment too long. She turned away but then noticed that her hand was on his arm. She removed her hand and then leaned back in her seat, placing her hands in her lap.

What was happening to her? She had just been gazing into Ian's eyes, wishing that she was his and he was hers. She'd told her girls that she wasn't attracted to him in a romantic kind of way. And Surry had thought that was true, but Ian was just too handsome, kind, magnanimous, and, and, and…she was losing it. The man was winning her over without even trying. Maybe she should have stayed at home.

If she had stayed home, she wouldn't be on this airplane discovering how much she and Ian had in common. For she had also allowed her parents' paths to lead her. By the time Surry was thirteen, her father had owned three failing dress shops. He could never find a way to make his shop profitable in order to take care of his family, and he'd refused to give up dreaming and get a nine-to-five where he collected a paycheck from employers who had their finances together. She just hoped she wouldn't end up like him, dreaming of success that would never come.

By the time they arrived at the Hilton hotel in the uptown area of Charlotte, North Carolina, Surry was so thrown off her game by thoughts of her father's failures and Ian's triumphs that she had to get away.

Ian looked at his watch and said, "I have a meeting at one this afternoon. So, I'm free for about an hour and a half. Do you want to grab lunch?"

"I need a little rest."

"Okay, well, then how about dinner when I'm done with my business today?" He waited a moment. When she didn't answer, he said, "Come on, Surry, you have to eat, and we still have a lot to discuss."

"Okay, I'll meet you for dinner," she told him and then escaped to her room. Ian was getting to her, and she had to find something to take her mind off this fabulous man whom any woman should be so lucky to have in her life. She sighed at the thought and then turned on her laptop and checked a few emails.

After that she spent another half an hour fiddling around in her room, and she got hungry. But Surry was too stubborn to call Ian, so she contacted room service and ordered a turkey club sandwich. While eating her sandwich, she looked through the hotel directory for things to do in uptown Charlotte, which most people called downtown.

A block over from the hotel was a NASCAR Hall of Fame Museum, but Surry wasn't much into cars. The directory also mentioned a Levine Museum of the New South. But this museum featured a lynching photography exhibit that was on display until December 31 and a permanent exhibit on the cotton fields. Surry didn't have the stomach to view either of those exhibits at this point in her life, so she continued her search for something to do in uptown Charlotte.

Then she ran across information on the Harvey B. Gantt Center for African-American Arts + Culture. That sounded like the perfect way to spend the afternoon. So she jumped in the shower and then changed into a pair of black slacks and a purple blouse with a loose-fitting silver chain around her waist. She put on sensible black shoes, since she would be walking to the museum. On the way out of her room, she grabbed a light jacket, because even though it was late November, it was about seventy degrees outside. Surry was pleasantly surprised to see that the uptown area of Charlotte was kept rather clean. But that might have to do with the fact that the banking industry was big in Charlotte.

The museum was displaying an exhibit titled "America I Am: The African-American Imprint." She was excited to see this exhibit, because it was about the achievements of African-Americans over the past hundred years. She also liked the fact that Tavis Smiley had pretty much developed this display. The exhibit spanned more than ten thousand square feet. Within that space were more than two hundred artifacts and other documents that provided perspective on the ways in which African-Americans helped to shape the economic, sociopolitical, cultural and spiritual atmosphere across America. As far as Surry was concerned, that was something to shout about.

Of course Martin Luther King Jr. was prominent within the display. But what made this exhibit unique was that music star Prince's guitar was on display in the "America I AM" exhibit also. So was the very typewriter that Alex Haley used to write his Pulitzer Prize winner, *Roots.* Rare artifacts were in the exhibit. The exhibit also included a life-size picture of the inauguration of Barack Obama, the first African-American president. Standing in front of that picture, Surry reflected on the feeling of euphoria she'd had when President Obama was elected and reelected.

Then her thoughts turned to the men and women who helped President Obama get where he was. The nameless faces of those people would probably never end up on a wall like this, celebrating history. But those people mattered. People like Ian Duncan made a difference in this world. And if she had designed this exhibit, she would have included pictures of the kingmakers, as well.

Surry took her time walking through the rest of the exhibit, making sure to study as many of the displays as possible. She was having the time of her life, feeling as if she were in her element at this exhibit. Before leaving the museum she made sure to tour the John and Vivian Hewett Collection of African-American Art. It was a permanent exhibit, but Surry had no idea when she would return to Charlotte, so she made sure to take in this collection that took the owners fifty years to gather.

After viewing the exhibits, Surry went back to the hotel and took a thirty-minute nap. She then put on her two-piece leopard print swimming suit, threw on the hotel robe and went swimming. The pool was deserted when she arrived, so she got in and began swimming, enjoying the solitude. She was on her third lap when someone jumped in the pool with her. Surry kept her head down and strokes strong as she swam the length of the pool.

She lifted up, putting her elbow on the edge of the pool as she wiped the water from her face. She then turned around to see who was coming up behind her like an underwater torpedo. The man was a strong swimmer, and Surry admired that. Since she hadn't started swimming until the age of twenty-one when she'd finally gotten tired of seeing others having fun in the ocean, she didn't consider herself a strong swimmer, but she was good enough to hold her own.

The man was swimming over to her corner of the

pool. As she was trying to decide whether to get out of the pool or move over so she wouldn't be in the way, he stopped swimming and stood up.

"Ian," she said, surprised as she watched him wipe the water from his face.

"You were expecting someone else?" he asked as he made a few steps in the pool and then bent his head down and allowed his lips to lightly touch hers.

Was this really happening? Was Ian kissing her? His lips felt so good that she couldn't help but put her arms around him and pull him closer. She opened her mouth and hungrily kissed him until she imagined herself purring with pleasure. "Mmm," she said with her eyes closed as the kiss ended.

Leaning into her, Ian kissed her eyelids, her forehead, her cheeks. He placed another soft kiss on her mouth and then said in a husky voice, "I could kiss you all night."

Her eyes popped open. Oh, my God, what had she done? She pushed him away and jumped out of the pool. "I'm going to get dressed for dinner."

"Don't go. I was just beginning to enjoy myself," Ian called after her.

With hands on her hips, she turned back to face him. "You were enjoying yourself a bit too much. And I'd appreciate it if you don't let it happen again." With that she swung around and left the pool area with as much dignity as she could muster.

Chapter 6

Ian knew that he shouldn't have attacked Surry in the pool. He had planned to get in and swim with her—nothing more. But something in him wouldn't let him back away once he stood up in the pool and saw how beautiful she looked standing there in that leopard-print bikini.

He'd been worried about her all day, since he'd called the hotel looking for her at least three times. She hadn't answered the phone once, and he wondered where she'd taken off to. Surry was such an independent woman that she never would have even thought about calling him to provide details about her outing.

Kissing her was his way of claiming some part of a woman who refused to be claimed by any man. But no matter why he did it, he had been wrong, because Surry hadn't wanted what he wanted. If she had, she wouldn't have stormed off like that. So, as he got out of the pool and went to his room to dress for dinner, Ian admonished himself to keep his hands off.

Once Surry was dressed, Ian took her to the hotel restaurant, because he didn't want to spend too much time out and about with Surry tonight. Ian needed to focus and not live in a make-believe world, thinking he was out on a date.

But by the time the salads were brought to the table, the two were communicating easily once again. Ian told her, "I looked up a few things that I thought you might want to do in the area. There's an African-American museum somewhere downtown. I can get us some tickets and take you over there tomorrow if you'd like."

"Thanks for thinking of me, Ian. But I already went to it earlier today."

"I should have known," he said with a look of disappointment showing on his face.

"I'm sorry, Ian. I hadn't thought to ask if you wanted to go."

"No, you wouldn't have," he said as he stuffed his mouth with salad.

Surry put her fork down. "What's that supposed to mean?"

He swallowed his salad. "It's not an insult. You're

just the type of woman who doesn't mind being alone. I just need to remember that."

The waitress stopped at the table with their plates. Surry took her chicken and veggies, and Ian was handed steak and potatoes.

Before eating a bite of her food, Surry leaned closer to Ian and said, "I don't like going places by myself. I've just gotten used to it."

He wasn't going to let this woman get to him. If she wanted to see, be and do everything on her own, then fine. "Look, let's just concentrate on what we're here for. Now, on the plane yesterday you mentioned that you give ten percent of your earnings to Haiti to help rebuild the schools. I'd like to do a press release concerning your giving. How does that sound?"

Her nose scrunched. "I don't know. Why do we have to tell everyone where my contributions go? Do I also have to tell everyone how much I pay in tithes to my church?"

"No, I'm not asking you to provide info on all your charitable giving. I just think we can get some positive press for you about this Haiti thing." He knew he was sounding testy, but he couldn't stop his voice from betraying his feelings.

Surry put her hand over Ian's and said, "I really would like to hang out with you while we're in Charlotte, Ian. I'm not just saying that."

He hated that she was able to read him so well, but he wasn't about to play games and pretend that he didn't have a problem with what she'd done. "Are you sure you want to hang out with me, because if you don't I can give you your space."

"I mean it. I'd love it if we could find something to do this week."

"Well," he said while pulling two tickets out of his jacket pocket, "I do have tickets to the Charlotte game tomorrow night. Do you like basketball?"

"Are you kidding?" She grabbed the tickets out of his hand. "I love it. I used to play ball in high school. But I wasn't tall enough for college ball."

Ian shook his head. How could he have so much in common with a woman who wanted nothing to do with him? "Then it's settled." His hands hit the table. "I'll pick you up in your hotel room tomorrow evening." He wasn't needed at Governor Monroe's until noon, but he wasn't going to ask Surry to spend her morning with him. At this point he just wasn't interested in the rejection that might bring.

They sat together eating their dinner, peppered with a few questions here and there that Ian threw in, as he was still trying to get a handle on the best way to present Surry's image. He wished that people could see this smiling, vibrant and animated woman seated before him.

He loved who Surry was when she forgot to hold up her guard and just allowed herself to relax. She became this free-spirited, giving woman whom he hungered to spend more time with.

"Why are you looking at me like that?" Surry asked.

"Oh, I was just enjoying the way you describe your exploits in Ghana."

"I can't help it," she said. "I love Ghana's story, because they have been through so much. The gold the land possesses made them a prime target for other nations who wanted to claim some of it for themselves. But the nation kept fighting back. Even after they won their independence in 1957, they still experienced several coups and have finally, within the last twenty or so years, become a stable nation."

"Just goes to show what people will do to be free. Me personally, I have a great deal of respect for our ancestors who refused to settle for slavery or the forty acres and a mule offered to some after slavery. We are definitely a people who can rise above circumstances."

"Hear, hear," Surry said as she raised her glass and did an air toast.

Surry couldn't remember a time when she'd enjoyed herself more on a dinner date. Technically, she and Ian weren't on a date, but she'd never wanted to be on a date more than she did right now. The man was exactly what she'd hoped to one day find. Why he had come into her life now, when she couldn't afford any distractions while building her company, was something she didn't understand.

She wasn't getting any younger, and yes, she would be thirty in three months. But did that mean she needed to drop everything she had worked so hard for and start rounding up men who might be candidates for marriage and fatherhood?

They had lingered at the table two hours after dinner. The servers were now looking at them cross-eyed, so Surry said, "I think we should probably clear out."

Ian glanced around. As he turned back to Surry, he asked, "Where'd all the people go?"

"Probably back to their rooms to get some sleep. We're the only ones crazy enough to sit here all night."

"You're probably right." Ian placed his MasterCard inside the card holder that had been lying on their table for some time. The waitress quickly picked it up and brought it back to him. Ian signed the bill and left a hefty tip. He stood and stretched.

Surry stood. "That was delicious, Ian. Thanks for inviting me to dinner."

"You flew here with me. The least I can do is feed you." He grinned as they headed for the elevator.

"You do know that I can feed myself, right?"

"Surry, I have no doubt that you can do any number of things."

She gave him a sideways glance, trying to figure out where that comment was coming from. The elevator opened, they stepped in and Ian hit the button for the seventeenth floor. Surry put her hands on her hips. "What was that crack about? Do you have a problem dealing with a woman who can handle her own business?"

He looked exasperated as he said, "I don't have a problem with it at all. Matter of fact, you can buy breakfast in the morning if it would make you feel better about having to accept a meal from me tonight."

The elevator opened and they walked down the hall. Surry felt like a bit of a jerk for being so unthankful about what Ian was doing for her. It was just that for years she had convinced herself that she didn't need anyone, because all her life, she never had anyone she could depend on. They arrived at her room and Surry stuck out her hand and said, "It's a deal. Breakfast is on me in the morning."

Instead of shaking her hand, Ian backed up and said, "Sleep tight, Surry. Don't let the bedbugs bite." Ian then went to his door, which was right next to Surry's.

"Very funny," she said. "There better not be any bedbugs in my bed or I'll be screaming the bricks off this building."

He unlocked his door and looked back over his shoulder at Surry. "Good night, lovely lady. I'll see you tomorrow."

"See you in the morning," she reminded him and then went into her room, sat down on her bed and began checking her voicemail. There was a call from her mother, two calls from reporters and a frantic call from Brenda Ann, the woman she left in charge of her boutique.

Worrying that something terrible had occurred at the boutique, Surry quickly called Brenda Ann. The woman answered on the third ring. Surry could hear the groggy sound in her voice as she said, "Hello."

Looking at her watch, Surry saw that it was almost midnight. "I'm sorry for waking you, Brenda Ann, but I wanted to check in with you tonight."

"Surry, thank God you called me back."

"You sounded pretty frantic in your voicemail message. What's going on over there?"

Brenda Ann cleared her throat. "We had some problems at the boutique today."

"What happened?" Surry questioned, eyes growing wide with concern.

"We had a shoplifter, but I caught the woman before she ran out of the store with the merchandise. I wanted to beat her like she had stole something, but I knew I would be turning Ms. Sticky Fingers over to the police, so I just hemmed her up until the men in blue came and took her for a ride."

Surry breathed a sigh of relief. "Is that all? You did great, Brenda Ann. Thanks for taking care of that."

"I wish that was all. I wouldn't have to bother you while you're on vacation if that was all. But unfortunately, we had bigger problems than that. Reporters have been calling here all day long trying to talk to you about John Michael and his claims."

"Two reporters left messages on my phone, as well."

"I think you should talk to them and set them straight," Brenda said and then sighed as she reported, "Another woman also came into the store. Instead of shoplifting, she just started taking pictures of several of the dresses. I didn't know if she had something to do with that John Michael so I ran her out of the store, as well. But I thought you should know about it."

"Thanks, Brenda. And you were right. I would have wanted to know about this." They hung up and Surry paced the floor, trying to figure out what to do. After wracking her brain for a while, she decided to call Ian.

"Miss me already?" Ian asked when he answered the phone.

"Some strange things are going on at my boutique and I wanted to get your take on it, if you have a minute."

"What's going on?"

Surry sat down on the king-size bed in her hotel room and recounted the story that Brenda Ann delivered to her.

"So you mean to tell me, on the same day that someone tried to shoplift, another person also tried taking pictures of some of your clothes?"

"And to top that off," Surry added, "reporters have been ringing the store all day long. Two of them called my phone also."

"What were the reporters' names?"

"I don't remember. I saved the calls on my voicemail. Do you think I should call them back?"

"No!" he screamed into the phone.

"Brenda Ann thinks I should call them and set them straight." She heard him grunt and then quickly said, "I'm not going to say anything crazy. I just think that Brenda may have a point. Those reporters are going to keep calling until we give them the information they're after anyway, right?"

"They will keep calling, but it's my job to handle them, not yours."

She took the phone away from her ear and looked at it. When she put it back to her ear she asked, "Why are you being so testy about this?"

"Sorry about that, Surry. I'm not trying to be rude to you. I just don't want you speaking to reporters and inadvertently saying something they might take the wrong way. Then instead of fixing this problem, we will have a whole other problem on our hands."

"All right, Ian. You're more experienced with this, so I won't call them back."

"Thanks," Ian said, breathing a sigh of relief. "Email me the names and phone numbers of those reporters and I'll talk with them first thing in the morning."

"I'll do it right now."

"You did the right thing by calling me, Surry. Now, don't even spend time thinking about this stuff tonight. Get your pretty little self some rest. I'll check into this and find out why these reporters are trying to get in touch with you. That way we'll know if anything new has developed."

"Thanks, Ian."

Just before they hung up, Ian said, "I meant what I just said, Surry. I don't want you to spend another second worrying about this. I'm on the job, and I plan to get this resolved for you."

"Okay. I'll talk to you in the morning."

"I'm going to need to take a rain check on breakfast. I'll take that time to try to figure out what's going on."

"That's fine, but I'll buy the snacks at the basketball game. How's that?"

The sound of his voice was labored as he responded, "If that will make you happy, Surry, then buy me all the snacks you want."

"Okay, see you tomorrow." As they hung up, Surry breathed a sigh of relief. Ian told her he would take care of the matter, and she believed him. But as she lay down and pulled the covers over her body, Surry realized that she was beginning to depend on Ian more and more each day. Whether that was a good or bad thing, she just didn't know.

She drifted off to sleep hearing her mother say, *"You can't trust a man to do nothing. If you want it done right, do it yourself."*

Chapter 7

"You're doing a marvelous job, Ian. I'm just grateful that no one else had snatched you up before I called," Governor Monroe said as they were wrapping up their work for the day.

"I am grateful that I was able to take the job. There's no greater opportunity than working on a presidential campaign."

Monroe patted Ian on the shoulder. "You say that now. But I know your type. You are much too loyal to leave a client just because something better came along."

Loyalty was the one thing his father had stressed to him, before their working relationship fell apart, and Ian had learned that lesson well. If he took on a client, it was because he believed in that person enough to go all the way with him or her. "You're right about that, Governor. But since we had just finished a campaign, I was available."

"I watched that campaign. You handled everything just right for Noel. I don't mind telling you that I was impressed."

Ian felt like asking questions…such as, why had Monroe bothered to pay attention to a congressional race when he had his eye on the presidency? But he let the thought pass as he considered the saying "Don't look a gift horse in the mouth."

"Are you bringing your lady friend to the luncheon?" Monroe asked.

"I'll check with her tonight to make sure that she's available."

"Well, if she isn't, my niece is still available," Monroe said with a wicked grin on his face.

The first day he met with Monroe, the man's niece had been in the office. Reese Monroe was a beautiful and refined woman. But she wasn't for him, so he quickly told Monroe that he'd brought a woman with him. "I'm sure that Surry will make herself available, but thanks for thinking of me." Ian left Monroe's office, hoping that Surry hadn't already made plans of her own for tomorrow.

He was completely exhausted after his day with Governor Monroe. They had stargazed until his eyes crossed. Monroe was a very intelligent man whose heart and soul bled for this country. Ian was convinced that the man would make a great president. And after spending several days discussing Monroe's platform, he was convinced that he wanted to manage Governor Monroe's campaign.

The work was just beginning. Monroe had asked him to move to Charlotte, because his campaign would be headquartered here. Ian had no problem with relocating from Houston to Charlotte for the next four years. He was single, owned his own company and had enough money in the bank to live anywhere he wanted. However, there were times, including now, that Ian wished it wasn't so easy for him to just pick up and relocate. He sometimes wished he had a wife waiting at home, someone who was going to argue with him about his travel schedule and how much time he wasn't spending at home.

But life was what it was.... Ian knew he was blessed and really had no room to complain, but after watching one friend after the next jump the broom into wedded bliss, Ian was now wondering about his turn. He had hoped that Surry would give him a chance. She was the kind of woman he needed. She was just as motivated and ambitious as he was. She wouldn't be sitting at home counting the minutes until her husband arrived. No, Surry would be out making her own way in this world, and he had a feeling that when they came home and spent their moments together...those would be the best moments of his life, causing him to want more than moments. Yeah, Surry was definitely the kind of woman who'd get a man off focus. Like now.

Even though he was dead on his feet, he'd promised Surry a night out. So, after leaving Monroe, he mustered up the strength to pick her up and take her to the Charlotte basketball game as they had planned. As he sat in the stands with Surry, watching her cheer, boo and make catcalls, he found himself being rejuvenated.

Surry stood up and yelled at a player who'd just had a ball stolen from him. "Hey, big boy, lay off the cookies and you might be able to get down the court faster."

Ian laughed so hard he just about choked on his Pepsi. He pulled Surry back down to her seat. "Some of these players are my friends. You can't heckle them while you're with me. They will never get me seats to the game again."

"You shouldn't have fair-weather friends, Ian. Besides, I'm a fan, so I have a right to call it as I see it, right?"

Ian shrugged.

Surry then stood back up and cheered a player on while he dribbled down the court, "Go, go, go, go." She lifted her arms and yelled, "Yeah, that's the way to do it!" as the ball swished into the net.

Ian found himself up on his feet cheering as if this was a championship game and a player had just scored the winning point. Their excitement had evidently been electrifying, because a whole group of other fans stood and cheered the player on, as well.

They all sat back down and continued to watch the game. It was getting good. One minute the score would be tied, and the next the opposing team would be up a few points. Then the Charlotte would bring it and tie the score up again.

"You told me that you liked basketball, but I just thought you were being polite," Ian said.

"Am I embarrassing you?"

Ian shook his head. "No, no. Do your thing. But if one of the players wants to fight after the game, I'm going to expect you to knuckle up and help me out."

She balled her fists and positioned herself like Rocky Balboa. "I got your back."

"That's good to know," Ian said, smiling up at her.

She sat back down and asked, "So, what's your favorite team?"

"Los Angeles, baby, all the way."

She shoved him. "You traitor. What's wrong with Houston's team?"

"I like your hometown spirit. But I have to admit that I'm a transplant. My family has lived in so many places that I'm just thankful that I still pledge allegiance to the good old U.S. of A."

Their attention turned back to the court as the Charlotte had the ball with a chance to tie the score again. The player took his shot and missed. Surry jumped up and screamed, “My grandmother could have made that shot, even as she steadied herself by holding on to her cane.”

The player turned toward the stands, gave Ian an evil eye and said, “You need to control your girl, man.”

Before Ian could stop himself, he got a mischievous grin on his face as he told the player, “When you control your aim, I’ll control my girl.”

The player shook his head and pointed at Ian. “No more tickets for you, my friend.”

Ian leaned back in his seat and laughed so hard this time that he had to stop the tears from rolling down his face.

When the game was over, Surry got an “oops” expression on her face. “Sorry about that. I guess I forgot to tell you that I’m one of those rabid fans. I get a little crazy when I watch the games.”

“You might have said something about not having any home training,” Ian joked as he stood and held out a hand for Surry. “Ready?”

She took hold of his hand as he gallantly held it out for her. If he had been any other man, Surry probably would have ignored the offer and stood on her own. But this was Ian. He’d been so good to her, even when she hadn’t shown appreciation. So, she didn’t want to pretend anymore. She needed his help and was grateful to have it. Ian had spent all morning working on her issues with John Michael, and she hadn't even thanked him for his efforts. Well, that kind of behavior would stop now.

They walked down Trade Street, holding hands as they headed to the hotel. Surry squeezed Ian's hand and softly said, "Thank you for helping me. Sometimes it's hard for me to admit that I need help, but I want you to know that I appreciate everything you're doing for me," she told him as they walked to the hotel.

"You don't have to thank me. But it does make it seem like you have a little bit of home training, the way you're being all nice right now. So, I'll be sure to tell the fellas that you aren't all crazy, just some crazy."

She nudged his shoulder. "Forget the players. I was just livening up the game." She got serious and added, "I just want you to know that I appreciate whatever you might be able to do. When John Michael first started spewing his lies, I didn't know what to do or whom to turn to. But my greatest fear has been that I might lose everything I've worked so hard to build."

Ian told her, "You let me worry about John Michael. When I'm done with him, I guarantee he'll be begging for your forgiveness."

"I don't want him hurt, Ian. So if you have anything like that in mind, just forget it."

They made a left on Third Street. With the hotel in sight, Ian had a grin on his face as he said, "Who do you think I am…the Mafia? I don't do physical violence, but trust me when I tell you, I still have ways of making grown men cry when it's necessary."

Ian had said those words with such conviction that Surry believed each one. He was a power broker, and men like that sometimes had more power than those they helped. If anyone could solve her problem, it was Ian Duncan. She wanted to wrap her arms around his neck and kiss him, but just as the thought occurred to her, they were standing in front of the hotel, preparing to go their separate ways.

"I'll walk you to your room," Ian said, still holding her hand. As they walked, he told her, "Governor Monroe is having a luncheon tomorrow and he's invited you. Is that okay?"

"How did he even know anything about me?" Surry asked suspiciously.

"He doesn't know about you per se. Monroe just knows that someone is here with me, but he doesn't know your name. Does it bother you to be associated with me?"

"Not in the least. I just wondered how the governor knew that you had someone with you."

"If you must know, Monroe tried to introduce me to his niece, but I told him that I came with someone and that you wouldn't appreciate me spending my time with any woman but you while we're in town."

"Using me to get the women off your back, huh?" Surry teased.

"You don't mind, do you?"

"Not at all, and I'd love to attend the luncheon tomorrow."

He pointed at her. "No heckling the governor. Okay?"

She released his hand to cross her heart. "Promise. I'll be on my best behavior."

He took her hand back as they continued to walk. Surry looked down, noticing the way their hands melded together. He was bringing her warmth and shielding her from the cold within, causing her to feel things she hadn't felt for any other man she'd dated. And for some reason she couldn't totally fathom, she was delighted that he hadn't wanted to entertain any other woman. "Ian?"

"Yeah?" he asked as they got into the elevator, heading to their rooms.

"I know that I can be a bit uptight, but I want you to know that I'm beginning to feel comfortable with you. It normally takes me much longer to get to this level of comfort with any of my friends."

His eyes were smiling as he said, "Woman, did you just relegate me to the friend zone?"

The elevator door opened, and as they walked to their rooms, Surry tried to explain. "That's not what I meant. I was just trying to tell you how—"

They were at Surry's door. Ian turned to her and said, "Just shut up and kiss me."

As he strode toward her, Surry stepped back until

she found herself against the wall…nowhere to run, nowhere to hide. But the funny thing was, she no longer wanted to run or hide. She wrapped her arms around him and closed her eyes as their lips met in sweet, blissful passion.

When their lips parted, Ian put his hands on the wall, close to each side of her face. He stared at Surry with heated eyes and then said, "I don't kiss my friends like that. Do you?"

Barely able to form a complete sentence, Surry shook her head.

"So we might need to find a new word in the dictionary to define us, huh?"

She nodded, knowing full well that he was dominating her mind and she was powerless to stop him. He lowered his lips to hers once again, and she shamelessly received him. She wanted the kiss to last, but when he stepped back she didn't try to stop him.

"I'll pick you up at eleven in the morning," he told her.

Her mind was so fuzzy, she didn't understand why he was offering to pick her up tomorrow. He must have seen something in the expression on her face that told him that she didn't know what he was talking about, because he added, "The luncheon at Governor Monroe's place? You said you would attend with me, remember?"

"Oh, yeah…yeah. I'll be ready."

"Thank you, Surry." He stood in front of her for a moment, inhaling deeply. "See you in the morning."

"Good night, Ian." Surry opened the door and floated into her room. She put her purse on the dresser and caught a glimpse of the goofy grin that was plastered on her face. *What in the world was Ian doing to her?*

What in the world had he allowed Surry McDaniel to do to him? He hadn't laughed this much in the past ten years. Surry did something to him when they were together. She brought out his silly side and amused him beyond what any other woman had been able to do. Surry was just so at ease in her own skin. She didn't pretend to be someone she wasn't.

The basketball game tonight proved that Surry was going to beat to her own drum, no matter who was watching. He'd never dated a woman who dared to yell at a bunch of almost seven-foot-tall men without once thinking of backing down. Surry was amazing. And the way he felt when he held on to her hand was almost electrifying. He hadn't wanted to let her go. He'd enjoyed the game, but the hand-holding had been the best part of his day. That is, until their mouths met.

When he kissed her, it was as if their souls danced together. She was the woman for him, and Ian knew it as he'd known nothing else. The only problem was that Surry wanted friendship from him rather than the relationship that Ian so desperately needed from her.

As he went to bed that night, Ian decided that it was best for him to cut his losses. He had too much work to do in the next four years to be chasing after someone who was so clearly unavailable to him.

"Keep your hands off Surry, from this day forward," he told himself.

Chapter 8

At eleven on the dot, Ian knocked on Surry's door. As he heard her footsteps, he reminded himself of his declaration from last night, but then she opened the door and blew all of his willpower away.

Her hair hung down her shoulders in curly waves. She wore a full-length, formfitting dress with black and white horizontal and vertical lines through the length of it. It was V-necked in the front and back and had a long slit up the back and angled bell sleeves. The dress took his breath away.

"It's a Cleopatra knit."

"And you look like a queen in it."

She twirled around, giddy as a schoolgirl. "Do you really like it?"

"Baby, I love it. I'm just wondering how I'm going to keep my hands off you in a dress like that."

Putting her hands on the fabric, she said, "I designed it for the woman who wants to feel like a queen for a day."

Ian's mouth was watering as he told her, "You hit the mark. I just hope that Monroe didn't invite too many men to this luncheon. "There is such a thing as too much male attention."

"Let me grab my purse. I left it in the bathroom."

Ian took the seat in front of the desk in her room. He needed a moment to get his thoughts together. How on earth was he going to be able to concentrate with Surry standing within a twenty-mile radius of him in that dress?

"Ready?" she asked as she floated back into the room.

No, not at all, he wanted to confess, but he put his man pants on and stood up. "Yeah, let's go."

The luncheon was being held at the ex-governor's home on the south side of Charlotte. Ian and Surry got in his rental car and then jumped on Interstate 77. The traffic was bumper to bumper, and it took forty minutes to drive fifteen miles. Along the way, Ian passed one three-car pileup, and couple of minutes down the road there was a five-car accident.

"What's up with the drivers in the city? This is the South. Shouldn't these people be more relaxed rather than running over each other?"

"A lot of New Yorkers and New Jersey folks have relocated to Charlotte."

"So you think it's the transplants to the city who are down here causing all these accidents?"

"Could be. I mean, this is kind of crazy." Surry pointed to a spot on the north side of 77. "Look, there's another accident."

Ian's focus was now on being careful as he drove this stretch of highway, but he still couldn't get that dress Surry was wearing off his mind. "So…is this the only dress you have that makes a woman feel like 'a queen for a day'?"

She shook her head. "I developed lots of dresses with the feel of royalty. I actually call it my Nubian Princess line, and it was this line that attracted the department store chains to my designs."

"How well is the Nubian Princess line doing in your store?"

"I haven't started selling them in the store yet. I designed them for the chain stores because they wanted something different. The dresses are beautiful, so I just hope the deal will still go through."

"Trust me, you don't have a thing to worry about."

Surry glanced over at Ian with wonderment dancing in her eyes. "Ian, you don't know much about the fashion industry, yet you sound so confident you're starting to make me believe that everything will turn out all right."

He nodded. "In my world, it's not what you know, but whom you know." He winked at her. "I got this."

She smiled and leaned back in her seat.

They made it to Monroe's grand residence, got out of the car and headed for the door. The butler answered. Ian whispered in Surry's ear, "How would you like to have one of those?"

Surry shook her head. "Too formal."

The butler welcomed them in and pointed them toward the parlor. And Surry continued, "I don't care how much money I make, I think I'll always answer my own door."

"I guess I know what not to get you for Christmas."

Ian grabbed hold of Surry's hand as they walked into the parlor. Monroe and his wife, Barbara, were standing close to the entrance. Monroe turned slightly toward the entrance and then his eyes did a double take. Ian grinned. Monroe was probably thinking the same thing he was thinking.... Surry was going to be the most beautiful woman in the room.

"Well, my boy," Monroe began, "I guess I see why you didn't need my help with that matter we discussed."

"That's right, sir, I think I've got it covered," Ian said, turning to Surry. She grinned back at him, handling the charade beautifully. He then turned to Barbara Monroe and said, "Mrs. Monroe, I'd like to introduce you to my date, Surry McDaniel."

Barbara held out a hand for Surry. "I'm Barbara,

dear. And where on earth did you get that divine dress?"

Surry shook Barbara's hand and opened her mouth to respond, but Ian cut her off.

He turned to the governor and said, "Before we answer that, Surry, may I introduce you to Governor Monroe. He led the great state of North Carolina through a revitalization period that brought the banking industry to Charlotte and aided in the growth this state is now experiencing."

"He has to say those nice things about me," Monroe said as he held out a hand for Surry. When she took it, he added, "Very nice to meet you. Now I see why Ian's eyes light up when he speaks of you."

"Is that right?" Surry asked with a sideways glance at Ian.

"Uh, Mrs. Monroe, back to your question." Ian lifted Surry's arm, allowing the Monroes to get a full view of the dress. "Surry is a designer. She made this dress herself."

"You don't say." Barbara put her hand to her cheek. "I've never seen anything so elegant. What is the name of your dress shop?"

"Designs from the Motherland, but I'm located in Houston."

Barbara's face dropped. "That's too bad. I don't get out to Houston much."

"Don't worry," Ian assured her. "Surry's designs

will soon be in stores all over the U.S. We'll keep you posted."

"But until that time, I could mail you a catalog and I can just send you whatever you see that you like."

"Perfect."

Two other guests arrived, so Ian and Surry made their way around the room. "I think you made Barbara's day."

"Are you kidding?" Surry whispered in Ian's ear. "Having her wear my designs while she and her husband are out campaigning…she just made my day."

"Do I at least get a peck on the cheek for introducing you?"

"Ian, you don't have to make up reasons to receive kisses. I kind of like kissing you. So, I'd be more than happy to do it again. But not right now."

He looked at her for a moment, stunned at the fact that she would admit even the slightest attraction she had for him. But kissing was a long way from wanting a commitment, so he still didn't know where he stood with this woman. So he simply nodded. "I'll get back with you on that later this evening."

"Ian!" A woman waved from across the room.

Ian's and Surry's heads swiveled in the direction of the beautiful woman headed their way. "Is that the governor's niece?" Surry asked with a scowl on her face.

The woman was in front of them before Ian could answer. She said, "I've been trying to get with you since our first meeting. My uncle wants the two of us to work very closely—" her voice purred as she talked "—on this project."

Surry hooked arms with Ian. She was almost glaring at the woman standing in front of Ian as she asked, "What project are you and Ian working on?"

"It's highly classified," she said, still looking at Ian. "I really couldn't discuss it with you. Sorry."

Feeling a bit uncomfortable with the way Reese was dismissing Surry and with the way Surry was glaring at Reese, Ian positioned himself in the middle of the women as he held on to Surry's hand. "Reese, I don't believe you've met my date, Ms. Surry McDaniel."

Reese gave a quick hello to Surry and then turned back to Ian and boldly asked, "So, when do you think you'll be back in Charlotte...alone?"

Ian felt Surry's nails boring into the fleshy part of his hand. "I don't plan to come back...alone," he answered, and then the pressure of Surry's nails subsided.

"Have it your way." Reese flipped her long hair over her shoulder and then strutted off like a woman who'd been told of her beauty one too many times.

Surry kept her voice low, but she let Ian know how she felt. "That was rude."

"A little," Ian admitted. "But you didn't have to draw blood." He lifted his hand and rubbed the spots where Surry's nails had dug in.

"Sorry about that. I was trying to remain on my best behavior like you asked me to, but that woman really ticked me off." Surry's eyes were squinting with anger.

"I appreciate that you kept your cool. Now, just know that I'm not off fooling around by day and dating you at night."

Surry turned a cold shoulder to him. "It's really not my concern what you do with your time."

"Mmm, that's why I'm in need of stitches."

Surry laughed. "Stop being a big baby. I didn't dig my nails into your hand that bad." She then pulled his hand toward her, turned it over and saw the marks she'd made. Surry then lowered her head and kissed the marks. "There, does that make it all better?"

Ian was speechless. Surry had done it again. In a room full of people, she managed to make him see only her. He wanted her all to himself, and he didn't know what to do with his feelings because he was so tired of being overlooked by this woman. Ian didn't know if he was imagining things, but she seemed to be into him. She had certainly softened since their first few interactions. But would she reject him at this point?

Had she really just kissed Ian's hand? Was she losing her mind over this man? What was wrong with her? Where was her pride? She was the one with the "queen for a day" dress on, but if she was kissing Ian's hand, she might as well bow down to him and be done with it. Turning slightly this way and that to see if anyone saw what she'd done, Surry caught a glimpse of Reese glaring at her. But no one else seemed to be paying them any attention.

She put Ian's hand down and stepped back. Clasping her hands together, she asked, "So, when do you think lunch will be served?"

"Barbara will be seating us soon, I'm sure." Ian glanced around the room and then turned back to Surry. "Do you mind if we mingle? I see a few people that I need to speak with and hopefully arrange a meeting or two."

"For when you come back to Charlotte?" Surry tried to ask as nonchalantly as possible, but in truth, she had been shocked when Reese mentioned that Ian would be back in Charlotte. But she really didn't know why she was shocked, because if Ian was going to be working with Governor Monroe, it only made sense that he would live where Monroe lived. But the thing that bothered Surry even more than the fact that Ian would possibly be living in Charlotte, was the fact that it mattered to her.

They walked around the room, making small talk with city officials. Ian collected business cards and passed his out. Ian was in his element, having a good time and making connections. They sat down for lunch and once it was over, Ian was back on the networking game. That grin on his face was priceless as far as Surry was concerned. That was the reason she noticed the minute it left and Ian's eyes became cloudy and unreadable.

She turned toward the entrance, where Ian's eyes had been focused, and watched as an older gentlemen walked in with swag to match his swag. He was slapping hands and passing out cards just as Ian had been doing. Surry noticed something else also. The man looked like an older version of Ian.

Seeing the astonished look on Ian's face, she leaned into him and whispered, "Do you know that man?"

"Unfortunately, I do." With that, Ian strode off in the direction the man was headed.

It looked to Surry as if there was about to be a massive collision, worse than anything they had witnessed on Interstate 77.

Chapter 9

"Ian, my boy, look who's here," Monroe said as he and Walter Duncan stood slapping each other's backs like long-lost friends. "I've been begging this guy to come and see me for months. He decides to show up the week you're here."

Now Ian knew why he was "boy" and "young man" with Monroe. It wasn't his age. It was because Ian's father was pulling the strings. And if a man needed his daddy to pull strings for him, he might as well be called a boy.

Ian stepped up to them. He looked from Monroe to his dad. "Is there something that you two want to tell me?" Ian asked as he tried to hold on to his cool.

"No, no, son." Walter patted Ian's shoulder. "I had

some business to attend to in Charlotte. So, I thought I'd come over and check you out. You don't mind your old man being here, do you?"

"Not at all. Knock yourself out." Ian walked back over to Surry, put his hand on the small of her back and whispered into her ear. "Do you mind if we leave now?"

Looking up at him, she smiled sweetly. "I'm ready whenever you are." Ian began walking her out of the room. Surry pointed toward Monroe. "Don't you need to tell him that we're leaving?"

"I'll get with him tomorrow." Ian rushed her out of the parlor. They made it as far as the front door before their escape was halted by Ian's dad.

"Son," Walter said as he came into the foyer, "are you going to leave without introducing me to this lovely woman?"

Ian rolled his eyes heavenward and then turned to face his father. "This is Surry McDaniel." Ian pointed toward Surry and then said, "Surry, this is my father, Walter Duncan."

Surry and Walter shook hands. "Nice to meet you, sir."

"It's my pleasure," Walter said. "Since Ian left home for college, I never get a chance to meet any of his ladies."

"Surry and I are just friends, Dad, so just leave it alone, okay?"

Walter gave Surry a suggestive grin as he said,

"If my Ian is fool enough to let you get away, he's no son of mine."

"Same old Dad, huh?"

As if remembering something he'd long forgotten, Walter's eyes widened as shame crossed his face. "I didn't mean it like that, Ian."

"Yeah, I'm sure you didn't. I've got to go." He grabbed hold of Surry's arm and walked out the door.

Walter held on to the doorknob as he told Ian, "I'm staying at the Ritz-Carlton. If you'd like to talk, come see me."

Ian kept walking. There was nothing for him to say to his father. He just wanted to get away. Everything had been going so well. He had the woman he wanted on his arm, the game-changing job and the respect of his peers. Then his father walked in the door and he was nineteen and feeling like a failure again. Why the man would interfere in his life now when he was making it happen on his own, Ian didn't know.

"What happened in there?" Surry asked once they were in the car and headed back to the hotel.

"I'm good." He had a stranglehold on the steering wheel and a scowl on his face. "Do you need anything before I drop you at the hotel?"

"You're not coming in?" Surry asked as if he were dropping her at her home in Houston.

"I need to clear my head. I'm going to drive around the city for a little while." He put his hand against his head as he squinted. "I think I need to pick up a pain pill also."

Surry opened her purse. "I have some Tylenol. When we get to the hotel, I'll get you a bottle of water before you go off on your drive."

"Don't put yourself out on my account."

Surry's eyebrow rose at that comment, but she kept her voice level as she said, "I don't mind helping you, Ian. I don't want you driving all over town with an aching head."

She sounded as if she actually cared about him. On another day, Ian would have analyzed that. But he just didn't have time to wonder about his love life when his career was falling apart. He pulled up to the hotel.

Surry jumped out of the car and left her passenger door open as she said, "Don't drive off. I'll be right back with the water." She hurried into the hotel, asked the desk clerk for a bottle of water and then ran back outside and jumped in the car. She handed Ian the bottle of water and then gave him two pain pills. "Take these."

"Look at you, being all bossy and acting like somebody's nurse or something."

"Just take the pills, Ian."

He took them, handed her back the bottle of water and said, "Thanks."

"All right, so will I see you later?" Surry asked.

"I'll be back around six to take you to dinner."

"Sounds good." Surry got out of the car and headed back into the hotel as Ian drove off.

Down the street at a stoplight, Ian took out his cell phone and called his father. When Walter picked up, he said, "I need to see you now. I'll be at your hotel in an hour."

Surry was confused by what had transpired this afternoon. One minute he was commanding the room, taking names and collecting numbers, and the next thing she knew, he was sulking and blowing people off.

Crazy thing was, she didn't care which Ian she was dealing with. Surry liked them both and wanted to be with him whether happy, sad, sulking or mad. Maybe she needed a shrink because she truly didn't understand the hold this man had over her.

Her phone rang, pulling her away from her thoughts. It was Danetta. "Hey, girl," she said when she answered.

"Are you watching the news?" Danetta asked excitedly.

"No, I just walked into my hotel room. What's up?"

"Turn it on. John Michael is on CNN."

Surry picked up the remote, turned the television on and then channel surfed to CNN. "I don't see him."

"It's on commercial. They showed John Michael's picture a few minutes ago and said they had further information concerning the fashion industry scandal that broke last week."

"He's probably just spewing more lies."

"It's back on. Hush, let's listen," Danetta said.

John Michael's short and balding figure was standing in front of a podium. He held on to the sides of it and leaned into the microphone. "Thank you all for coming. I'll be brief."

"Who dressed this man?" Surry asked as she spotted the skunklike jacket he was wearing.

"Hush, girl, let's hear what the tacky little man has to say."

"I'm sorry for wasting everyone's time," John Michael began. "But Surry McDaniel did not steal any of my designs. My assistant was simply mistaken in bringing the matter to my attention. Again, I apologize about all of this."

John Michael then turned and walked away from the podium while reporters screamed unanswered questions at him.

Surry's mouth was hanging to the floor.

"Why would John Michael take the word of his assistant without checking the matter out himself?" Danetta asked.

She picked her jaw up and said, "He's just lying. There was no assistant making accusations. It all came from John Michael, and now he's trying to save face."

"Assistant or not, I wonder what made him change his mind so fast?"

Surry knew exactly why John Michael had changed his story. It's not what you know, but whom you know, Ian had said. And as sure as she knew her name, Surry knew that Ian had found a way to get to John Michael.

"Ian did it," Surry said proudly while clapping her hands as if she'd just seen an awesome performance and needed to respond in kind.

"What did Ian do?"

"He took care of things for me. That man has got some skills." Surry was sounding dreamy and she knew it, but she couldn't stop feelings that she'd kept bottled up for so long from filling her heart. She could trust Ian. He was a man of his word.

"It sounds like somebody is a wee bit infatuated with a certain campaign manager who shall remain nameless."

"Girl, go on and name him. And tell me what kind of spell this man has cast on me while you're at it. Because I can't stop thinking about him," Surry confessed.

"And just think, you didn't even want to give the man the time of day a couple of weeks ago."

"I've just been so busy trying to get my business off the ground that I didn't have time for a relationship."

"And now you do?"

Danetta had just asked the million-dollar question,

and Surry didn't even have a two-dollar answer for her. Ian had said that having love and success was the best of both worlds. At the time, Surry had thought that Ian was just being naive. But now she was beginning to believe that love and success probably was the best of both worlds for men, because they didn't have to give up anything. In most family units, the woman had to rush home to cook, and the woman gave birth and stayed home with the children.

Men continued on with their lives while women made all the sacrifices. Her mother had sacrificed her career to help her father with every failed dream he ever had. She had thought being with the one she loved would make her happy, but in the end she ended up bitter and unsatisfied.

But her friends had found men who were successful and motivated. Neither Ryla nor Danetta had to give up her career just because she fell in love. Both of them were now pregnant, and she hadn't heard either of them talk about leaving the workforce. So, where did that leave her when she was so focused on building her dreams? After thinking all that over, Surry finally opened her mouth and answered Danetta's question. "I don't know, but I think I'm ready to find out."

"Surry, you and I have been best friends for a long time. I know just about everything there is to know about you. But I've never understood why you're so afraid to let yourself go and just fall in love."

"I would love it if I had time for the kind of love you and Ryla gush about. But I'm too busy trying to build my career. You were a partner in the advertising firm that you and Marshall own when the two of you hooked up, so your career had already been built," she reminded Danetta.

"Ryla had just started her event planning business when Noel came back into her life. She didn't push him away and tell him to come back when she was rich and successful," Danetta countered.

Surry got off the couch and went over to look out the window. Her room had a view of the front of the hotel. She was hoping to catch a glimpse of Ian driving back. "Yeah, but Ryla and Noel had a seven-year-old child. They owed it to Jaylen to go on and get married, especially since they still loved each other."

"I don't know, Surry. I just want you to be happy. And from everything you and Ryla have said about Ian, he seems like the man for you."

Surry closed her eyes for a moment and exhaled. "We have so much in common, Danetta."

"I know, I know…he's a student of black history, too. Two nights ago you told me about his Haiti trip."

"It's not just that," Surry began. "Ian and I are alike on so many levels." She didn't want to blast him out, so she didn't tell Danetta about the obvious rift between Ian and his dad. But Surry had been thinking about it all afternoon, because it pretty much paralleled the rift she had with her own father. Oh, Surry in no way deceived herself into believing that Ian was upset with his father because he had been a terrible provider as Surry's dad had been. The parallel came in the fact that they both had issues with their father. Maybe they could go to therapy together.

Before they hung up, Danetta implored her friend, "Do me a favor, Surry. Give yourself a chance with Ian. I think he might be the one."

After she hung up the phone with Danetta, Surry paced the floor, trying to get her mind right. Here she was in her hotel room preparing to wait an hour for Ian to pick her up and take her to dinner. She'd never waited so much as fifteen minutes on a man in her entire life. But this was Ian, and he was perfect. But did she have time for a man in her life, even one as perfect as Ian?

As she was pondering this issue, her cell rang again. This time it was her mother. Surry was drained with thoughts of Ian and really didn't want to go through another episode of "Your Dad's a Loser" at this moment. But she hadn't returned her mother's call from a couple of nights ago, so there was no way she could ignore this one. She picked up. "Hey, Mom, how are you doing?"

"Not so good, honey. Your dad is on another one of his harebrained schemes, and I'm about to lose my mind."

Here it comes. Now she was expected to ask, "What's he working on now?"

"This maniac wants to expand his clothing store. Never mind that the current one is already sucking us dry.... We wouldn't be able to pay our bills if you didn't send us money every month. But please don't mention that to your father. I handle the books for his stores, so he doesn't know how much money we aren't making." Sylvia McDaniel released a frustrated sigh.

"Why don't you tell him, Mom? Maybe he'd stop making all these rash decisions."

"Are you joking?" Sylvia let out a bitter laugh. "Your father has jumped from one poorly executed business to the next. He doesn't care if we don't have the money. Willy believes that the fairies will sprinkle their magic dust and the money will just appear."

Surry had her issues with her father also, but her mom was being a bit harsh. "Mom, I remember seeing some of the business plans he came up with when I was a kid."

"Oh, you mean like the plan he constructed for the hair salon and supply store combo that went bust after only two years? Or what about the time he allowed a man he'd known for a week to con him into becoming the proud owner of a grocery store that was about to be foreclosed on? Or what about the time—"

"Okay, Mom, I get your point. Your husband is a bad businessman." Could this conversation just be over? Surry ran her hands over her face and began massaging her temples as a headache emerged.

"It's not that your dad is so bad with business.

But he won't stick to anything. It's like, this week he'll want to be an astronaut, but next week he'll decide that he really needs to be president of the United States...and he hasn't bothered to gain the skills he'll need for either job, you know what I mean?"

Yeah, Surry got it. Her dad was a bum and irresponsible in the way he dragged his family from one dysfunctional dream to the next. "Do you need me to send some more money, Mom?"

"Oh, no, dear, you hold on to your money. I want you to have enough to save for your future. What you send now is plenty enough for us."

"Okay, well, just let me know if you need anything."

"I will, but that wasn't the reason I called," Sylvia said. "We got to talking about your father so quick that I forgot to tell you that I saw that evil old John Michael on television."

"I just saw him, too."

"He looked like a little skunk. Did you see that white-and-black jacket he had on? The man has no style. I kept wondering why in the world you would steal his designs. They have to be the most god-awful things on planet Earth."

"He's a liar, Mom. As I told you before, I didn't steal any designs from him, nor would I ever."

"I'm just glad he's finally told the truth. I would die of embarrassment if everyone thought my daughter was a thief."

Surry wanted to laugh. She truly loved her mother, but the woman had just as little faith in her as she had in her father. Surry felt as if she'd spent a lifetime trying to make up for her father's failings. But nothing was ever good enough. Sylvia picked on everything she did. But the things she said to Surry were nothing compared with the way she talked about the men Surry dated. She spoke loud and clear about everything she hated about her dates. But most important, men trying to find themselves were not good enough for her daughter and needed to keep on searching elsewhere.

When Surry had been in her early twenties, she'd tried to explain to her mother that it was natural for men of that age to not know what they wanted to do with the rest of their lives. Her mother had said, "That's what college is for. If he hasn't a clue what he wants to do now, then he wasted his parents' money. And mark my words, Surry, he will make a waste of his life."

She'd stopped mentioning her dates to her mother, and as the years progressed Surry had found herself dating less and less. But now Ian was in her life, and she wanted her mother's approval of this man so desperately that she said, "Ian helped me out with that little crisis. I doubt John Michael will be lying on me ever again."

"Who is Ian?"

"A man I met." A wonderful man, actually.

"Is he at least a gentleman? Successful?"

"Absolutely."

"Well, just make sure he has his head screwed on right and isn't out there still trying to *find himself.*"

"Maybe I'll bring him by so you can meet him. Then you'll see for yourself that Ian is the real deal." Surry hung up the phone, confident that she had finally found a man whom she'd have no trouble introducing to her demanding mother.

Chapter 10

Ian stormed into the Ritz-Carlton and made his way to his father's room with anger in his heart. The warm hues and rich wood tones in the lobby did nothing to soothe Ian's mood. Twelve years ago his father threw him off a senatorial campaign he'd been helping out with while in college.

He and a few coworkers from the campaign had accepted a lunch invitation from the media. Ian got cozy with a beautiful woman reporter who'd shown interest in him. Before he knew it, he'd inadvertently let the senator's whereabouts slip out. That reporter then went to said location and found the very married senator soliciting sex from a male prostitute inside a men's bathroom.

Ian had profusely apologized to his dad for ruining the campaign, even though it was the senator's bathroom sex that was to blame. Ian never found out how she managed to sneak in the men's bathroom. But it didn't matter, he'd still blown it big time.

His father had been livid. He'd called Ian incompetent and a few other choice words. Ian had been distraught over his father's anger, but the thing that had ruined their relationship from that day forward was what Walter Duncan had said next.

"You are a total screwup, Ian. I hope you know that you've cost us this election."

"I think that Senator Rance cost us this election when he decided to have bathroom sex with someone who wasn't his wife." Ian put up a finger as he added, "Oh, and lest I forget, who also happened to be a man."

His father wouldn't let up on him. "You had no business giving that reporter any information about the senator's whereabouts."

Ian sat down and covered his head with shame. "I know that, Dad, and I have apologized profusely for my mistake. But I can't take it back. We just have to move forward and worry about damage control and the next campaign right now."

Walter shook his head. "Allowing you to continue playing this game of following in my footsteps will ruin me. You obviously don't have what it takes to be in this business if you can't even keep your mouth shut when you're talking with reporters."

"But I'm not just following in your footsteps, Dad. I love this business just as much as you do." Ian had tried to plead his case.

But Walter wasn't hearing it. He shook his head. "This was a mistake. You're fired, son. Don't bother coming back to the office. Oh, and I'd change your major from political science to business or something, because you'll never get a job on another campaign."

Walter Duncan had left his son bruised and wounded that day. But Ian hadn't changed his major. He figured that if his father was right and no one would ever hire him to work on a campaign, he could teach in college or write books about politics. He would have done just about anything to remain in this game he loved.

But the one thing Ian would not do was accept charity from a man who didn't believe in him from the start. Ian had been making his way in politics. He would have eventually gotten the golden goose without his father's help. But Ian knew exactly why Walter had decided to butt in where he wasn't wanted. He knocked on the door and prepared to unload.

Walter opened the door, looking as dapper as ever in his double-breasted navy blue suit with a silver silk tie, holding a wineglass in his hand. He held it up to Ian and said, "Congratulations, son, I've been hearing such good things about you."

Ian closed the door behind him and sat down on one of the comfortable chairs in the sitting area. He opened his mouth and told Mr. Johnny-Come-Lately, "I have made a successful career in politics without your help. So, I'm trying to figure why in the world you thought it was okay to interfere in my life at this stage in the game."

Walter walked over to the seating area with a confused look on his face. "I'm not interfering in your life. I don't know what you're talking about."

Ian wasn't going to let his father get away with playing dumb. He pointed at his father and said, "You got me Monroe. I know it and you know it."

Walter sat down in the chair opposite Ian's. He put his wineglass down. "Son, I wasn't trying to interfere in your life. I saw an opportunity for you and simply floated your name. That's it."

"Isn't it funny how 'son' just rolls off your lips, as if you cared anything about your family."

"Look, son, I may have made some mistakes, but I've never stopped loving you. Nor will I ever stop being your father." He picked up his wineglass and took a gulp.

Ian wanted to pitch a fit in this room, to just start yelling and screaming in his dad's face. But the truth was, his father wasn't worth the anger. So he turned to the man, looked him square in the eyes and said, "I haven't needed charity from you since I was nineteen years old. I'm dropping Monroe as a client. You can take him if you think he's so great."

"Don't do this, Ian. You've got a once-in-a-lifetime opportunity here."

Ian stood. "You worked on presidential campaigns three times in your lifetime. Another one will come around for me."

Ian started for the door.

Walter followed. "You're good at what you do, Ian. Don't squander your gift just because you're still mad at me after all these years."

Ian swung around, fire in his eyes. "Oh, now, that's rich coming from you. A man who stomped on his own son's dreams. I don't have what it takes to be in the business. Remember that, Dad?"

Pain etched across Walter's face as he admitted, "I was wrong, son. Can you please forgive me?"

"I wish I could forgive you. And I'm not buying this performance you're putting on." Ian swung open the door and then turned back to his father. "This is all about ego building. The only reason you want to help me is because you know I'll eventually get the kingmaker campaign on my own. But you can't stand the thought of that, can you?

"Oh, no, not the great Walter Duncan. You're not satisfied with being known as a kingmaker. Now you want to interfere in my life so you can puff out your chest and tell the whole world that you're also the maker of kingmakers. Well, not this time, Dad.

"You fired me when I was nineteen. Well, now I'm telling you to take this job and give it to another puppet, because I don't want it." With that, Ian left the building.

Ian had a dinner date with Surry at six. But he wasn't ready to go back to his room and get dressed. He needed to clear his head and relieve some tension before he picked up Surry.

Soaking in the garden tub, with vanilla-scented candles providing a shimmering light in the bathroom, Surry picked up her e-reader and began reading a romance novel that she had started last week but hadn't been able to finish with so much going on. If Danetta and Ryla knew that she filled her e-reader with romance novels, they'd probably laugh and call her a hypocrite.

But Surry wasn't a hypocrite. She believed in love. She just didn't know if there was a forever kind of love out there for her. So, she read her romance novels and lived vicariously through other women who resolved their issues and found a way to make love work. She didn't read steamy romances. Some of the stuff in those books was TMI as far as Surry was concerned. She preferred the sweeter romances...boy meets girl, boy likes girl, girl likes boy. Boy holds girl's hand, kind of like the way Ian held her hand the other day as they walked back to the hotel from the basketball game.

Holding hands with Ian wasn't electrifying or mind-blowing as described in novels, but it nonetheless felt good and right. Her hand fit just right inside his. Surry also enjoyed when the hero and heroine shared their first kiss. In the novels she read, that first kiss was always like magic, or like Christmas morning.

A grin spread across Surry's face as she admitted to herself that her first kiss with Ian had been more like the Fourth of July, with fireworks and combustible energy. Kissing Ian made her feel the way she had the first time she'd ever kissed a boy, without all the which-way-do-I-turn-my-face, nose-bumping awkwardness.

Surry managed to make it to the end of the chapter, even though her mind had been on Ian the entire time. She turned off her e-reader, figuring she had soaked long enough, especially since she had a dinner to get ready for. She soaped up and then drizzled warm water over her back to get the suds off. She then immersed the rest of her body in the warmth of the water to remove the remaining suds.

Surry jumped out of the tub, remembering to blow out the candles as she towel-dried. Wrapping the towel around herself, she went back into her living quarters and began making preparations for her evening with Ian. It was five-twenty. So she had less than an hour to find an outfit, work on beautifying her face and decide if she would be wearing her hair up or down.

Looking over her wardrobe, Surry decided she wanted to wear a pants suit tonight. And she knew the exact one. The pants were a solid purple with straight legs. But the jacket was the thing that gave this outfit sparkle. It was multicolored with purple serving as the base color. However, black and gold was sprinkled all over the jacket in abstract fashion. The jacket was formfitting from the shoulders to the belly button. But at the point of the waist, the jacket flared all the way down to the upper thigh. It was gorgeous and Surry knew she looked good in it.

Surry put on moisturizer and makeup and decided on an updo for her hair. She then put on her outfit and sat down on the couch, turned on the television and waited for Ian to knock on her door. Glancing at her watch, she noticed that it was now five minutes after six. She expected her men to be punctual when picking her up. But Ian had a lot on his mind when he dropped her off today, so she would let his tardiness slide this time.

"Hit me again," Ian commanded the bartender.

The bartender poured more scotch into Ian's glass and attempted to walk away. Ian grabbed the man's arm and said, "Leave the bottle."

The bartender gave Ian the once-over. "Haven't I already filled your glass three times?"

Ian leaned back in his seat, pulled out his wallet

and handed the bartender a hundred. "Leave the bottle," Ian commanded again.

The bartender hesitated. "Will you need me to call you a cab when you get ready to leave?"

Ian pointed upward. "I'm staying upstairs, so as long as I remain steady on my feet, I won't be needing any help."

Nodding, the bartender left the bottle next to Ian's glass as he put his Benjamin in his pocket and moved down the length of the bar.

Ian wasn't feeling so good about the way this day had turned out for him. He had been riding high on hopes and dreams, believing that everything was turning out just the way he planned it—although it wasn't how he'd planned it, because Ian never expected to run a presidential campaign so soon. He had already mapped out his career, and the way Ian saw it was that after he managed to get more positive press and more candidates elected, then he would be set to handle the next presidential campaign.

So he should have known something was fishy when Governor Monroe seemed to want him above all others. He gulped down his scotch and filled his cup again.

His cell phone beeped, letting him know that he'd just received a text message. He took his phone off the clip, preparing to check his text message, when a woman came up to him and asked if he had a light. "Don't you know that smoking is bad for your health?"

She pointed at the bottle. "Probably as unhealthy as drinking like a fish."

Ian laughed. "You might have a point there." He lifted his bottle. "Care to take some of this off my hands?"

"Don't mind if I do." She sat down. "I'm Peaches, by the way."

Ian looked at the woman. He thought Peaches was an odd name for a woman who had to be in her mid-fifties. But who was he to judge? If she wanted to be Peaches, then Peaches it was. "I'm Iaaaaan." His words were slurred and running together.

Peaches lifted a hand for the bartender. When she got his attention, she said, "Glass, please."

Ian poured a drink in the glass the bartender set in front of Peaches and then asked, "Are you here on business?"

"Yes, but my business partner and I handled our last meeting a few hours ago. I'm just waiting for her to get dressed so we can check out the nightlife in this city."

Ian was leaning over in his seat as he slurred, "Sometimes that nightlife is bad for your health, too."

Peaches giggled as she helped Ian sit back up straight. "You're a cute drunk, but I hope you're not driving away from here."

"Why is everybody so worried about me?" He pulled out the Hilton card key. "I'm right upstairs, so I won't be let loose on the road with innocent bystanders."

"Thank God," Peaches said.

Ian's phone beeped again. As he reached for it and read the text, his face contorted in shame.

"Forgot to be somewhere?" Peaches asked. "My ex-husband was an alcoholic. I spent a lot of time texting him and reminding him about events we needed to be at. Somehow he still managed to miss about half of the events, including our anniversary."

"I'm not that kind of man," Ian declared.

"Prove it." Peaches pointed at his cell phone. "Put that woman out of her misery and go handle your business."

"I don't know if she'll forgive me. I missed our date." Ian poured another drink and gulped it down. It burned his throat, but he shook it off.

"So you're just going to sit here and keep drinking. Careful, you're going to end up being an ex, just like my ex-husband."

Ian stood, wobbled and then held on to the chair. "Well, lady, I'm n-not y-your ex-husband, and I'm not a drunk." He handed her the rest of his scotch. "You and your friend enjoy the rest on me." He then turned and headed upstairs to try to make amends for what he'd done.

Surry was worried out of her mind. Why had she let Ian drive off in the condition he'd been in earlier?

She'd seen how disturbed Ian had been at running into his father, and he had a headache when he left. She should have offered to drive him around or something. At least that way she wouldn't be worried that he'd gotten hurt in an accident.

She'd already texted him twice and received no answer. That didn't seem like Ian, so Surry was pacing the floor, ringing her hands. Her heart was in the pit of her stomach at the thought of Ian being in danger.

She turned on the television and found a local news station. It was eight-thirty at night, but this station ran all day long. She watched and listened for a few minutes, hoping and praying that she wouldn't hear Ian Duncan's name as an accident or homicide victim.

After about fifteen minutes of news coverage, Surry remembered that Ian's father was staying at the Ritz. She decided to go over there to find out if he'd seen or heard from Ian. Maybe he would help her look for his son. She took off her outfit and changed into a simple black jogging suit and a pair of boots. She rushed to the door and swung it open.

Ian practically fell on her. She stepped back, holding him at arm's length as he waved at her like an idiot. "Hey, Surry."

She caught a whiff of his breath, put her index finger against her nostril and said, "You're drunk."

"Why does everyone keep saying that? I had a couple of drinks. That's all." Ian wobbled into her room and plopped down on her couch. He then looked up and gave her outfit the once-over. "You're going to dinner in a jogging suit?"

She wanted to strangle him. Nobody, not friend or foe, had ever stood her up or kept her waiting for over two hours and then showed up on her doorstep as if nothing was wrong, when it was obvious where he'd spent his time.

She closed the door and with hands on hips strutted over to him. She wanted answers. How in the world had a man she believed to be perfect pulled such a stunt on her? Had this been his plan all along…to make her want to be with him to the point that her heart was aching, and then abuse her by being so insensitive as to show up for a dinner date two hours late and full of booze? "You have a lot of nerve, Ian Duncan. What you have done tonight is inexcusable."

Ian didn't respond. He just kept his head low.

"I was so worried. I thought you'd been in an accident or something since you didn't even have the decency to respond to any of my text messages." Surry was practically shouting as she glared at him. The thing that was making her even angrier was that he wouldn't say anything back to her. He wasn't acting like her Ian. What was wrong with him? "Say something!" she shouted.

Ian slowly lifted his head. His eyes held so much sadness that it caught Surry off guard. He looked as if the world had just crashed down around him. In that instant she knew that something life-altering had occurred in Ian's world.

"I don't know what to say, Surry. I guess I'm still the same screwup I've always been."

Ian Duncan was a lot of things, but a screwup wasn't one of them. He was in pain. Surry knew instantly that his pain had been caused by his father. She was familiar with that kind of pain, because her father had been the source of her pain and fears. She had no clue how to help herself deal with the issues she had with her father, but maybe she could spend this night helping Ian.

Chapter 11

"It wasn't real…it wasn't real at all," Ian mumbled to himself as he sat on Surry's couch trying to come to grips with the way life would be for him from this day forward.

"What isn't real? What's wrong with you, Ian?" Surry sat down next to Ian and put her hand on his shoulder. "Talk to me, please."

"I'm the biggest fool in the history of politics."

"I doubt if that's true," Surry said as she began counting off political scandals and foolishness. "Sarah Palin looked foolish as she tried to step into shoes that were obviously too big for her to fill. And what about that Anthony Weiner, using Facebook to pick up chicks while his wife was carrying his baby?"

"Those were dumb mistakes, but both Sarah Palin and Anthony Weiner stepped into their own mess willingly. I had no idea I was being played. But I feel like a fool because I should have known if it looks too good to be true, it probably is." Ian slouched on the couch as he leaned his head against the headrest.

"Okay, you need some coffee." Surry jumped up, grabbed the phone and dialed room service, requesting a pot of coffee. She then looked over at Ian and asked, "I'm just guessing, but I don't think you had anything to eat yet, either, right?"

Had he eaten? His head was swimming so bad right now that he couldn't remember what he did two seconds ago, let alone an hour ago. But his stomach felt empty, so he shook his head.

Surry then said into the phone, "Can we get two dinners also?"

"Sure, what can I get for you?"

"This late at night, I'll take a grilled chicken salad." She looked over at Ian and added, "Can you bring a rib eye, medium well, and a baked potato with sour cream and chives, but no butter?"

Ian couldn't help but notice that Surry had asked for the exact piece of steak he'd ordered the other night, and she'd even ordered his baked potato the way he liked it. She was paying attention.

"We'll take whatever fresh fruit you have also." She put the phone down and came back to sit next to him.

He looked over at Surry. Her eyes were glowing with concern for him. Ian felt like the biggest jerk there ever was. "I've got to get out of here. I shouldn't be bothering you with my problems." Ian attempted to stand but lost his footing and fell face-first into the seat of the couch.

Surry pulled his head out of the cushions and then helped him sit back on the couch the right way. "You are not going anywhere. You've been unselfishly helping me with my business…by the way, thanks for whatever you did to get John Michael to recant his lies. So, now I am going to help you."

He mumbled something unintelligible.

"Just lean your head back and rest. The coffee will be here in a minute and then we can talk."

He leaned back and began talking to himself, "I'm not a man at all. I'm still my father's little boy." He then lifted his head and asked Surry, "Why do you even want to be friends with me? I'm nothing more than a disappointing little boy."

"That's not true. You're a full-grown man with potential and worth," she declared, speaking life into him.

"Men don't just follow in their father's footsteps." He grabbed hold of her arm and blew his hot breath in her face as he asked, "How can I ever expect to expand my path when Walter Duncan managed to get three presidents elected. I'll never work on that many campaigns in my lifetime. I might as well just give up."

She removed his hand from her arm and stood up. "You're just talking crazy now. I need to get some coffee in you quick so you can start talking like you've got some sense." Surry grabbed the coffeepot and was getting ready to make the coffee herself when a knock sounded on the door.

"Thank God." She put the coffeepot down and opened the door.

"I have the coffee you ordered," the waiter said.

Surry opened the door wide. "Thanks so much. Just set it on the table." Surry grabbed her purse and gave the man a tip.

"Thank you, ma'am."

"Not a problem. Enjoy the rest of your evening." The door closed and she poured coffee in a cup. She poured in two packs of sugar, stirred it and then handed the cup to Ian. "Drink this."

He didn't argue with her. She didn't seem as if she was in the mood to take no for an answer. He took a couple of gulps and then watched as she took the blanket off her bed and spread it out on the floor. "What are you doing?" he asked.

She looked up. "I figure you're too drunk to sit at the table and eat. So, I'm going to make us a picnic."

"Well, if I'm as drunk as you think, I could just fall over on the floor, too."

"That's why I put the blanket next to my bed. I'm

going to let you lean against the mattress until you get enough food and coffee in you so that you can sit up straight," Surry said.

She then gave him a smile that tore at his heart. How could he disgrace himself by coming to a woman like Surry in such a messed-up condition? How could he ever expect her to want to be a part of his life now? Trying not to depress himself further, he took another gulp of his coffee.

There was another knock on the door. Surry answered the door again. But this time Ian took a five out of his pocket and tipped the waiter.

Surry spread the plates of food out on the blanket and then helped ease Ian to the floor. He leaned his back against the mattress as she filled his cup with more coffee.

Ian took the cup from Surry and gulped as much of it down as he could. She sat down across from him and then handed him his dinner plate. "Thank you," he said.

Surry set her plate in front of her, dug her fork into her salad, took a bite and then said, "Okay, now we've got the coffee and some food for your stomach. Let's eat and talk so we can get you all fixed up."

"Good luck with that, 'cause it's going to be a long while before I'm all fixed up again." Ian took another sip of his coffee.

Surry put her hand on her heart as her eyes filled with something akin to sorrow.

"Don't look at me like that. I might be drunk, but you don't have to spread all this pity around."

"I just don't know what to say to you. When we left this afternoon, you were on top of the world. The luncheon was going well for you also—that is, until your father walked in. So, what happened?"

"My father is what happened." Ian took a bite of his steak to soothe his stomach and head. He was developing a headache and hoped that the food would relieve all his problems.

"I already know that your father has something to do with why you chose to get drunk tonight and stand me up, but I just don't understand. Your father seems successful, and you're doing the same kind of work. So I would think that the two of you would be swapping stories and trading secrets."

"That's what I had thought when I was young and idealistic. And then my father fired me, and those rose-colored glasses came off real quick."

With a look of surprise on her face, Surry dropped her fork and said, "Are you serious? Your father really fired you?"

"Looking back, I would have done the same thing to a staff member of mine who did what I did."

"What did you do?"

Ian told her about being nineteen with hormones flying and the cute reporter who tricked him into divulging information about their client, which cost them the election.

After he told Surry what the senator was caught doing, she said, "Yeah, I would have fired you, too… or at least suspended you until you got your hormones under control." Shaking her head, she added, "Men."

"Okay," Ian admitted, "I could handle being fired, especially because of what I did. But the things he said to me that day have bothered me for a long time. He said I had no place in politics and that I would never work on another campaign."

Pulling a few grapes off a stem, she said, "Well, you showed him, didn't you? I mean, not only did you help Noel win his election, but you are now getting ready to work on a presidential campaign."

"It's not real, Surry. My father got me this gig. He's playing some sort of sick game that I don't want any part of. So, I fired myself from this campaign. No need to wait on the old man to do it."

Surry's head swiveled. "You did what?"

"You heard me. I'm not taking Monroe on as a client."

"Just because your father had something to do with it?"

"Exactly!" He lifted his fork and twirled it around as if he'd finally found a kindred spirit, someone who gets him. "I won't be controlled by that man. If I can't get my own clients, then I don't need them."

Surry looked at Ian for a moment, opened her mouth, hesitated and then charged forward. "Maybe you're just scared—"

"I'm not afraid of nothing." Ian was practically thumping his chest with this declaration.

Surry lifted her hands in surrender. "Maybe I used the wrong word. I am simply suggesting that since you disappointed your father on the first campaign you worked with him on, you might have—" she spaced her index finger and thumb about a millimeter apart "—a teensy-weensy bit of fear about disappointing him again."

Ian's head was too fuzzy to process what Surry was trying to communicate to him. He'd eaten half of his steak and all of his potato. He was full and ready to sleep. But he didn't want to go back to his room. So he asked, "Do you mind if I lay on my picnic blanket? I need to get some sleep."

"Let me get you a pillow." She jumped up and grabbed two pillows off the bed and then found another blanket in the closet. She handed Ian the pillows.

"Thanks," Ian said as he lay down on the floor.

She bent down and put the cover over him.

He grabbed her arm, smiled and said, "I like the way you take care of me. Do you want to get married?"

Surry fell on her backside at Ian's words. Her hand went to her mouth as tears glistened in her eyes.

Ian might have been drunk, but what he'd said had come from the heart. He wanted to grow old with Surry. But he also knew that he had to take care of some things before he'd actually make her a good husband, so he said, "I really should have waited on that, huh?"

Surry took her hand down. "Did you mean it? Or is that just the alcohol talking?"

Ian took Surry's hand in his. "I've never wanted anything more in life than to be your husband. But it's not like I have a job. My career just blew up, and right now it seems as if I need to give some serious consideration to what I want to be when I grow up."

Her brows furrowed and she removed her hand from his. "You already have a career, Ian."

He waved that suggestion away. "That's my father's career. Maybe I need to become a professor or something. What do you think?"

She thought the same thing that had been ingrained in her since she was a child. No thirty-something-year-old man who was still trying to find himself was good enough for Sylvia McDaniel's daughter.

Surry sat in front of Ian, watching while he slept. He'd asked her to marry him. Even drunk, those words from Ian's mouth sounded like music to Surry's ears. But tears rolled down her eyes as she heard her mother say, *"He's still trying to find himself. Do you really want to hitch your wagon to a dreamer with no direction?"*

"He has direction," she tried to silently argue with her mother as tears continued to fall. She gently touched his hair and ran her hands down to the base of his neck. "You made me love you," she said to his sleeping form.

"Do you want to end up like me, a bitter old woman because of living in poverty with a dreamer?"

Still fighting this battle with her mom in her head, she silently said, "But I've got money. And once my contract goes through, I'll have even more."

"He'll squander it, Surry-girl. Listen to your mama. I've been where you're going...run, don't walk out of this man's life, and don't you dare look back."

Closing her eyes as another tear dropped, Surry got up off the floor, put her suitcase on the bed and began packing her clothes. Her mother had won the battle once again. She needed to go home and get as far away from Ian as possible.

Ian grunted, rolled over and then grunted again. His eyes flickered as they began adjusting to the morning light that was streaming into the room. He lifted an arm and yawned. As his eyes opened and he wiped the sleep from them, he realized that he was on the floor. "What in the world?" He got up and stretched his stiff body.

Ian then looked around the empty room. That's when he remembered that he'd stayed in Surry's room last night. "Surry!" he yelled.

When he didn't get an answer, he walked over to the bathroom, holding his pounding head. Ian knocked on the bathroom door. No answer. He checked the knob and found it unlocked. Opening the door, he peered in with a sneaky grin on his face. She wasn't there, either.

Ian turned around and then stood in the middle of the floor with fists on his hips and a perplexed look on his face. Ian tried to remember exactly what happened last night. As his eyes continued to roam the room, he noticed that her clothes were no longer hanging in the open closet and her suitcase was gone.

He grabbed his cell phone and dialed her number. When it went to voicemail, he said, "Hey, I'm in your room, but the funny thing is, you aren't here. Can you give me a call and let me know what's going on?" He hung up and looked around the room again.

"She left me. But why?" His head was killing him as he tried to put it all together. He sat down on the bed, rubbing his temples as a thought came to him. "I asked her to marry me last night."

Chapter 12

"Wake up and open the door, girl."

Surry heard the banging on her door, but she remained on her couch, hoping that whoever was there would just go away. She'd spent the entire night crying and wasn't up for company of any kind.

"We came over to celebrate with you."

It was her girls. Ian must have told Noel that she had left Charlotte, because both Ryla and Danetta had called first thing this morning. She hadn't answered, but she never expected them to show up at the house. Surry blew her nose and then wiped her eyes. She got up and opened her front door.

"Why weren't you opening the door?" Ryla asked as they walked in.

"I was asleep. But y'all kept banging on the door and woke me up." Surry went back to the couch, lay down and pulled the covers up to her shoulders again.

"What's going on with you? Why are you sleeping out here on the couch?" Danetta asked.

"Why so many questions? Can't I sleep wherever I want in my house?"

Ryla put her hands on her hips as she examined the living room. "Have you been crying?"

Surry hopped up and grabbed all of the used tissue she'd thrown on the table and the floor around her. "I'm just a little upset," she said as she rushed the tissue to the trash can in the kitchen. When she came back into the living room, Danetta and Ryla had removed her cover and were sitting on her couch, giving her the eye.

"We've seen you upset, Surry. But you've never cried until your eyes were puffy and red or been so disheveled—" Ryla pointed at Surry's hair and clothes "—as you're looking right now."

Surry couldn't help herself. The tears just kept coming, as unwanted as ever. Wiping them away again, she said, "I'm not having a good day."

"Ah, sit down and tell us what's going on." Danetta took hold of Surry's arm and seated her between her and Ryla. "This should be a good day for you, hon. John Michael recanted his lies, and I'm sure your contract will go through now without any problems."

"I know. You're right. But I'm not upset about anything John Michael did. This cuts so much deeper."

"Oh, honey, what's wrong?" Ryla put her arms around Surry and hugged her.

"I fell for him."

Her words came across as mumbles. Danetta handed her some tissue as she asked, "What did you say?"

Surry blew her nose again and wiped away her tears. "I'm in love with Ian," she shouted.

"That's no reason to cry. Ian is crazy about you. I've heard him and Noel talking, and trust me, Surry, you have nothing to worry about."

"I wish that were true, Ryla."

Danetta waved her hands in the air. "Hold on. I'm confused. When you and I spoke on the phone yesterday, it sounded as if you had come to terms with your feelings for Ian and you were happy about it."

"I was." Surry wiped the tears from her face again as she added, "Then Ian changed on me."

"What do you mean?" Ryla asked.

"I didn't know that loving someone could hurt this much," Surry said as she leaned her head back against the couch. Her friends were silent, allowing her time to get her thoughts together. "I'm sorry for acting like such a freak."

"Just tell us what happened," Danetta cajoled.

"He found out that his dad helped him get a client and he totally flaked out on me. Got drunk and started talking about giving up his business to become a college professor or something else. It didn't sound like he was sure what he wanted to do anymore."

"And?" Ryla questioned.

"And that's it. I can't be with someone who isn't serious about his business and wants to follow one new idea after the next."

"Ian is very serious about his business. He has been managing political campaigns since leaving college. From what Noel told me, this is the only job Ian has ever really wanted," Ryla told her friend.

"It sounds like Ian is trying to cope with some issues he has with his father," Danetta said.

"Aren't we all," Surry said bitterly.

The look on Ryla's face clearly indicated that she didn't understand what her friend was going through. "Surry, I don't mean to upset you, but it sounds like you bailed on Ian just because he had a bad day."

"My father put his family through a lifetime of bad days. He's always trying out new business ventures that do nothing but fail. My mother has lived a miserable life because of him."

"What does that have to do with you and Ian? He's a good man, Surry. Don't let him go like this."

"Ryla, I wish it was that simple. But I can't be with a man who has no direction." Surry jabbed at her head with her index finger. "My mom put it in my head that any man on a quest to find himself is just a bum like my father and he's only going to make my life miserable.

"I have tried so hard to stay away from men like that. I even stopped dating altogether because no one ever seemed to measure up to my mother's standards."

Danetta put a hand on Surry's shoulder. "You can't live your mother's life, Surry. What she and your dad had might not have worked, but that doesn't mean that Ian's going to make you miserable."

"Ian is passing up a chance to work on a presidential campaign, an opportunity he's worked his whole life to obtain, simply because he's mad at his father. If that isn't screwed up, I don't know what is."

"Yeah, but if you love this man, you need to help him figure out who he is during the good times as well as the bad," Ryla said.

Surry's head rocked from side to side. "I don't have time to fix anybody. I'm too busy trying not to live in poverty so I can continue providing for my mother."

"But you love him, Surry," Danetta reminded her.

"I don't know what to do. I can't deal with irresponsible, fly-by-the-seat-of-their-pants men."

"It sounds to me as if you first need to deal with the issues you have with your father and this fear you have of not being provided for," Danetta said.

"That's great armchair psychology. But I don't know what to do about my father, either."

Danetta said, "I have learned to trust God to see

me through any problem that I face. So, what I think we should do is pray about this situation."

Surry believed in the power of prayer, so she held out her hands so that she and her friends could join hands and pray.

Ian stepped into his office like a man on a mission. He'd allowed his father to turn him into a blubbering buffoon of a drunk. And Surry had ripped his heart out, after he'd gone so far as to ask her to marry him. He'd called her countless times, practically begging her to respond to him, but Surry wasn't answering his calls or returning his messages.

Ian needed to resurrect his career, so he didn't have time to chase after a woman who didn't want to be caught. The last thing he wanted was to look at Surry like a lovesick pup as that guy in the airport had done. He just hoped that a whole lot of work would ease the ache in his heart.

It was time for him to get back to being Ian Duncan, man of the hour. He had just helped Noel Carter win a congressional seat when nobody thought it was possible. He might have just dropped the next president of the United States from his client list, but Ian was prepared to find other clients. Last night, he'd lamented about finding another career. But in the light of day, he realized that he wasn't doing this just to follow in his father's footsteps. Ian truly enjoyed his career. He had an eight-year plan that was designed to move him in the circles he needed to be in to get that top political client. Ian wasn't a quitter. All he had to do was work his plan, starting now.

Seated behind his desk, Ian began reviewing notes on his iPad. Before Governor David Monroe contacted him, Ian had a list of six potential clients: one gubernatorial candidate, a senator up for reelection, three congressional races and one mayoral candidate.

The potential governor was gone; he'd found a campaign manager last week. The senator was still interviewing. From what Ian saw and heard about his last campaign, the manager had been arrested for soliciting a police officer, so the senator was being extra careful with his selection this time. Ian put a check mark next to his name.

Of the three congressional races, only one was a reelection. Guiding a candidate through a reelection was sometimes easier than introducing a new person to the field of politics. But Ian happened to know that the congressman would soon find himself defending a charge of misappropriation of campaign funds. Ian wanted nothing to do with it.

Even though he was interested in at least one of the two men running for Congress, those were still pretty much local races, so Ian decided to pass. The mayor, however, was a different story. He was Hispanic, a go-getter with political aspirations through the roof. After serving as the mayor of Houston, he planned to run for governor, and then he wanted to set his sights on the White House.

Demographics were changing in Texas, to the point where Ian actually thought that this particular politician had a shot at becoming governor…and then president of the U.S. of A. Ian put a check mark by his name and then said to himself, “Work the plan.”

He started making phone calls and setting up meetings. He didn’t need a handout. He was going to make his own success and change the world, one campaign at a time.

Chapter 13

After church on Sunday, Surry was supposed to do the normal brunch thing with her girls, but she was being led in a different direction, so she begged off and headed three and a half hours down Interstate 45. There was someone she needed to see in Dallas, and it couldn't wait another day.

She parked her car in the shopping center, got out and started walking to her destination. So many of the shops that had once lined the street were now gone, replaced by other businesses, and based on the traffic she noticed at this shopping center, it didn't seem that these businesses had much staying power, either.

Her father's dress shop was around the corner. As she turned the corner and headed for Mt. Blue—she had no idea where he came up with the name—Surry thought about the fact that she had left home ten years ago and hadn't talked to her father since except to say, "Can I speak to Mom?" He had failed her by not providing for his family and forcing her to depend on student loans to get through college.

The closer she got to her father's dress shop, the more her heart began to ache for the way she'd treated a man who'd done nothing but love her. After praying with Danetta and Ryla, Surry did some real soul-searching, and that search led her to the door she was standing in front of right now. Taking a deep breath, Surry stepped inside the dress shop. The shop was half the size of her boutique, but it was nicely decorated, and where other shops in this shopping center seemed empty, customers were looking around in her dad's place.

She didn't know how many of them were actually paying customers, but he was obviously attracting shoppers into his store. She wasn't sure how he was doing it, but, go Dad! Willy McDaniel was standing behind the cash register waiting on a customer. He looked up, glanced at Surry and then did a double take.

Surry was nervous. She didn't know how to act around her father. She waved and smiled at him, hoping that was enough to let him know that she wasn't here to start drama. He smiled back and then called to a young woman on the opposite side of the room.

She walked behind the cash register and took over for her father. He then rushed over and wrapped his arms around her.

"Surry! Surry! I'm so happy to see you."

It felt good to be in her father's arms. As she lingered, Surry finally realized that denying her father love had also played itself out in other areas of her life. She was generally uncomfortable around people and refused to allow anyone other than Danetta and Ryla into her inner circle. And her love life was a total mess. Surry ran from every man she'd ever been involved with.... Let him sound too much like her father, and she was out of there.

"Can I talk to you for a minute, Dad?" Surry asked as the embrace ended.

"I'll have as much time as you want in a few minutes. We're about to close up, so if you just let me finish with a few of these customers, we can grab some dinner and talk for as long as you like."

Surry nodded. "Sure, Dad. I'll just look around while I wait." She hated the fact that she felt uncomfortable around her own father. But ten years of barely speaking would cause a rift in any relationship. She stepped away from her father and began looking around the store. He had good taste, she could say that much for him. The dresses were quality material. Surry just wondered how long these outfits stayed in the store waiting on a buyer.

As she moved from rack to rack, Surry was surprised to discover that her dad had a section of Designs from the Motherland in his small store. Her mother had never told her that they were selling her designs. Surry wondered at that, and as she did she remembered how her mother had been ready to believe the worst of her in thinking that she had stolen those designs.

Her mother had wanted to be a designer, but had done little more than hem and sew clothes from patterns for her few customers. Surry hated to think it, but she was coming to the conclusion that her mother's unhappiness stemmed from her own failed dreams. Sylvia's lack of success caused her to turn a blind eye to the fact that her husband's business was obviously growing. Willy McDaniel had finally found the business he could succeed in.

That knowledge had caused Surry to feel proud that her father had kept on striving, trying out one business venture after another until he found the one that fit him. Why couldn't her mother see what was right in front of her?

A woman came out of the dressing room and rushed over to the cash register. "I love it. I've got to have it."

She put the dress down on the counter. Willy smiled as he picked up the dress and began ringing it up. "Once again, you picked the best dress in the house."

He told her the price. She pulled out her credit card

with a smirk on her face. "So I guess you're going to tell me that your daughter made this dress, too?"

"You know it," Willy said as he winked at Surry.

"I'd like to meet this daughter of yours one day. I hope she knows how much you brag on her," the woman said as she finalized her sale.

Surry was too stunned to move. As her father walked the woman and his assistant out, tears streamed down Surry's face. She had made her father an enemy instead of realizing that fear was her true nemesis. Her mother's constant belittling of her choices and her father's numerous business ventures had caused her to be afraid of failure. But now Surry knew that she didn't have to take her fears out on her father. She could pray and turn those fears over to God and keep moving toward success.

Her father locked up and then walked back over to Surry. He lifted his hand and wiped the tears from her face. "Why are you crying?"

"I'm so sorry for the way I've treated you, Dad. You've never done anything but love me, and I pushed you away." As each word fell out of her mouth, more tears flowed down her face. This reality was hard to take, because Surry was also coming to terms with the fact that she had pushed Ian away without giving him a chance to see his dreams flourish. Maybe politics wasn't his thing.... Maybe the next venture he tried would be for him and he'd be able to succeed at it.

"I'm not upset with you, Surry, and I don't want you to be upset with yourself, either."

"How can you say that, Dad? I am your daughter and I have dismissed you for ten years. You should be mad at me. I don't deserve your kindness." Surry closed her eyes, trying to block out the shame she was feeling.

Willy pulled her into his arms and held her tight as he said, "Don't you tell me how to feel or who to bestow kindness to, Surry McDaniel." He released her, looked her in the eye and said, "You're my girl and I love you."

This time Surry wiped her own tears away. "Thanks, Dad."

"Now that that's settled, let's go get something to eat." Willy went to the back and grabbed his jacket.

When her father came back to the front of the store, Surry said, "It looks like you're making a success of the store. What turned it around for you?"

Willy smiled. "About two years ago a distributor came into the store and showed me some of your designs. He had no idea that I knew you, but I recognized your handiwork immediately and started purchasing them for the store. Word began to spread about the fabulous and sleek designs I was carrying, and business has started turning around."

"Is that why you're thinking about expanding?"

"Gotta strike while the iron is hot," Willy said as he opened the door and they walked out.

An idea hit her and she turned to her father and said, "My store in Houston is doing pretty well. I'd like to expand also, but I'm going to be busy with a new deal I'm working on. So I'm wondering if maybe my father would be interested in going into business with his daughter."

"Oh, I couldn't afford to pay for a franchise at this point."

"Dad…" Surry gave him an are-you-serious look. "You wouldn't have to pay to franchise. You'll bring the years of expertise and the time to work the business and make it a success. I'll put up the capital." She stuck out her hand. "What do you say? Do I have a partner?"

"Do you really need me?"

"I've needed you for a long time. I was just too stubborn to know it."

Ian's meeting with Juan Manuel was going better than he'd expected. Juan hadn't found a campaign manager yet and was ready to get started. The special election for the mayor's office would be held in six months.

"This campaign means everything to me," Juan tried to explain.

Ian nodded. "I know how committed you are to the people in this community. They would be blessed to have someone like you running the city. That's why I want to help you pull your campaign together."

Juan wiped his mouth and placed his napkin on the table. "This is important to me because I want to do more for the community I've been serving as state senator for the last six years. I also plan to run for governor in the next election."

"You'll not only run, but with me as your campaign manager, you will win and be ready for a presidential campaign." Ian's confidence was on full display. "Trust me, Juan. I see your future, and one day the world will be calling you Mr. President."

Juan smiled. "How do you know whether or not I'm even interested in the presidency?"

"If I'm wrong, please correct me. I need to know whether I'm dealing with a future governor or a president, because that will determine the way I manage each of your campaigns."

"Let me put all my cards on the table." As Juan leaned back in his seat, he held the guise of a man destined for greatness. "I was skinny as a rail when I was a little kid, and do you know why?"

Juan was fit and athletic. Ian knew for a fact he was a runner, so he had a lean frame, but he wouldn't consider him to be skinny as a rail. Ian hadn't heard the story of Juan's super lean days. He put his elbow on the table and his fist underneath his chin. "Do tell."

"My family was so poor that other poor people looked down on us. We even qualified for food stamps, but not enough to feed us for the entire month. So, my brothers and I went hungry a lot." Juan hesitated a moment and looked as if he was trying to shake off an unwanted memory. "Anyway, you asked if I wanted to become president. And the answer is yes, but not for myself. I want to become president of the United States because I want to help lift up the poor. Politicians seem to be more concerned with the middle class or the rich, and they fail to see that the poor need more than food stamps and a medical card.... They need a hand up so that they can get a piece of the American Dream themselves."

Ian was impressed. He knew that Juan had a heart for the poor, because his platform in the state senate centered on them. But hearing the man speak about the issue allowed Ian to see the passion in his eyes. "I'm here to help in any way I can. I look forward to the day when you are seated in the Oval Office making decisions that will lift up the poor."

"Well then, let's go do it," Juan said as he held out a hand to Ian.

Ian shook Juan's hand as he nodded. "I'm ready." Ian handed Juan a folder. "We'll get started on the campaign for the special election right away. But I will also be working on an eight-year strategy to get you into the White House."

They talked for about another hour, finalizing details as Juan asked Ian to work with him on this campaign and the future ones to come. Ian felt as if he were walking on water when he left the meeting with Juan. The man had *it* and would shine like the sun on the campaign trail. Ian had hit the jackpot, and he hadn't needed his father's interference to make anything happen.

He got in his car and started the engine. Then as a thought hit him, Ian checked his cell phone for text messages or missed phone calls, hoping that Surry had finally returned his calls. There was no message from Surry, text or otherwise. He sighed as he threw his phone back in the passenger seat. He wasn't going to let this ruin his day. He would accept Surry's decision. She obviously didn't want to be in his life, so it was time to move on.

He made it back to his office building at about three in the afternoon. Ian had tons of paperwork he needed to go over and he needed to start building a team to work on Juan's campaign—and all of it needed to be done yesterday. But Ian enjoyed his job the most when it seemed as if he'd been thrown into the fire.

He opened the door to his building, and as he began walking down the hall to his office, he caught a glimpse of a woman in his waiting area. His heart dropped because he could recognize her silhouette anywhere, anytime. He stopped in his tracks and turned to face her.

Surry stood and walked over to him as if no daylight had passed between them. "Can I speak with you for a moment, Ian?"

He nodded and turned and started walking toward his office again. As Surry followed him, Ian knew in his heart that the fire was about to get ten times hotter.

Chapter 14

Surry couldn't read Ian's expression as she laid her heart open for him to stomp on it. He was sitting in his chair behind his desk, keeping as much distance from her as possible. "Believe me, Ian, leaving you in Charlotte was the hardest thing I've ever had to do."

He crossed his arms over his chest. "It didn't seem to be too hard for you. You didn't bother to return any of my calls. That told me right then that you didn't want to be bothered with me."

She walked around the desk, got on bended knee in front of him and prepared herself to beg if she had to. "I left because I was afraid of what loving you meant."

"How come you didn't answer any of my calls?

Why couldn't you just tell me that you thought we were moving too fast or something like that?"

She grabbed his hand and looked him in the face, hoping that her eyes displayed all that her heart wanted to say. "We're not moving too fast, Ian. I really care about you. I believe I'm falling for you."

Ian stood and strutted over to the window and looked out at the activity in the parking lot. He wasn't prepared to be all in, not if it meant getting his heart trampled on again. "What do you want from me, Surry?"

"I want you to give us a chance."

Ian didn't respond. He just kept looking out the window.

She sauntered over to him and put her hand on his shoulder. As he turned to face her, she said, "Remember when you told me that having love and success was the best of both worlds?"

He nodded.

"Well, I'm starting to believe that." She pointed at his chest. "You made me believe it. So, don't walk away from me now. Give us a chance to see where this can go."

Stepping away from her again, Ian sat down on his sofa. "I don't know, Surry. What if I get back with you and you pull that running stunt again…with no explanation…no phone call or nothing."

She sat down next to him. "I handled the whole situation wrong. I know that now. But I got scared when you started talking about switching careers. You sounded like you didn't have any direction, and I can't be with a man who bounces from one thing to the next."

Ian stared at her incredulously. "You mean to tell me that you left because I was having a moment of indecision?"

"Well, yes. I have been raised to believe that a man should know what he wants." She raised her pointer finger, mimicking her mother.

"So you think I'm just some fly-by-night kind of dude, with no direction for my life?"

The look in Ian's eyes told her she'd better choose her next words carefully. "I would never think that, Ian. I've seen you in action, so I know that you are good at what you do. But that night, it seemed as if you let your father get you off focus…and I have to admit, it scared me."

"Well, just so you know, I am very much back. I'm focused on my career, and I've even found a new client."

Surry jumped in her seat. "Oh, Ian, that's wonderful. Tell me about him."

With an air of pride, Ian said, "His name is Juan Manuel."

"I know Juan," Surry said. "He's our state senator, isn't he?"

Nodding, Ian said, "He's going to be our mayor in a few months. Then it's off to the governor's mansion."

"Well all right, Juan. He always seemed ambitious to me."

"You have no idea." Ian sat up straighter as he continued, "I think his future is very bright. The demographics are changing in Texas, and he makes an impression on everyone he meets."

"That's true. You see that I remembered who he was. And I've only seen him twice, I think."

Ian slapped his hands together, got up and stood behind his desk again. "I've got a lot of work ahead of me, so I need to get down to it."

He was dismissing her. She couldn't let that happen. She had to remind him about what he felt for her—that is, if he still felt the same way. "Ian, you asked me to marry you just last week. You can't expect me to believe that you no longer care about me." *Please say you care...please say you love me.*

"You left me, Surry." He shrugged. "I just don't know what you want from me."

"Your heart, you fool!" She was just about ready to pick up something and throw it at his head. "I've never asked that of any other man, so if you let me walk out of here, I'll be crushed, but I won't come crawling back." Her chest heaved with emotion as she stood there waiting for his response. She quickly said a silent prayer, but when Ian didn't say anything, she turned and started walking out of his life.

Ian had called her four times since she left him in Charlotte last week. She knew she should have returned one of those calls, but she had been busy trying to sort things out in her world. After seeing how much her father enjoyed working in his small dress shop yesterday, and realizing that he had found a way to succeed, Surry knew then that she could love Ian no matter what path in life he chose.

She'd come here to tell him that today, but he wasn't listening. And she couldn't continue to beg a man who already had his mind made up. But the hardest part about walking away from Ian was that she knew he cared. She could see it in his eyes. But if he was going to allow his stubborn pride to get in the way of their happiness, then she didn't want him.

She put her hand on the doorknob, turned it and took a step forward, preparing to walk out of his life.

Ian ran his hands down his face and let out a long-suffering sigh. "Wait!"

Surry sucked in her breath. She closed her eyes, said another silent prayer and then turned back to face the man she wanted to be hers. Calmly, she asked, "Do you have something else you want to say to me?"

"Yes," he said as he stepped from around his desk and walked over to her. He took her hand off the doorknob and closed the door. He stepped forward and she stepped back. Now her back was against the wall, and Ian put his hands on the wall and leaned into her as he said, "I'm not ready to let you go."

"Well, why didn't you say that before? You almost let me walk out the door."

"Shut up and kiss me." Ian lowered his head and claimed her as his own as he devoured her with his mouth.

This felt so right and so good to Surry. She and Ian belonged together, and she would never, ever leave this man again. She wrapped her arms around him and intensified the kiss until she was weak in the knees.

He pulled away from her then banged his head against the wall.

"What's wrong?" she asked, thinking he was regretting his decision to get back with her.

He groaned. "I would love to stand here and do this all day long, but the truth is, I've got to get back to work."

Surry took her arms from around his neck. "Get back to work, baby. You and I can get together later."

He looked over at the pile of work on his desk. "Let me get a few things off my desk and then I'll take you to dinner or something."

"Dinner sounds good." She was trying to keep the grin off her face, but failing miserably. After thinking that she would not be able to have the man of her dreams, here he was offering to take her to dinner.

"Okay, Ms. McDaniel." He bent down and placed a kiss on her forehead. "Figure out where you want to eat tonight, and I'll call you as soon as I'm done here."

"I'll be waiting."

"So, does this mean that you'll answer my calls from now on?"

"On the first ring," she said as she opened the door, giddy at what had transpired. "Now get back to work."

"I'll call you later."

"I'll be waiting." Surry was smiling from ear to ear as she made her way back to her car. Things were changing in her world, and Surry wasn't a bit nervous about it. She and Ian belonged together.

"What just happened?" Ian asked himself. Did Surry really just come to his office and confess to be falling in love with him? He'd thought it was over between them, and now suddenly he had another chance.

His phone rang. It was his office manager, and Ian was thankful for the call, because he needed to get his head back in the game. He answered the phone and said, "Ian speaking." That was his first mistake. His next mistake was listening to his assistant, and from there the day just got worse.

Before meeting with Juan, Ian had put together a list of venues and press junkets to get Juan out and about in the community. His assistant had been working on the package. The folder he'd handed to Juan this morning had his new schedule in it, which was one of the things that had impressed Juan. And now it seemed as though everything was falling apart.

Ian went into full command mode, calling in favors and putting his Rolodex to work like never before. During Ian's career he had rubbed shoulders with some of the most influential men and women in the city of Houston, the state of Texas and around the country. Today, he just needed to connect with his Houston contacts. Shouldn't be too big of a deal, he thought at four in the afternoon.

At nine forty-five, Ian was finally finished with all the changes that needed to be made. His desk was still full of work that he hadn't been able to get to, but he would have to tackle that tomorrow. He put his jacket on and headed for his car. As he was driving home, he thought about a hot shower and a good night's sleep. Then two thoughts crossed his mind… Surry and dinner.

How could he have screwed this up—again? The woman of his dreams was giving him another chance, and he'd just blown her off. He came to a red light and then picked up his cell and dialed her number. As promised, Surry answered on the first ring. He tried to lighten the moment by saying, "I thought you women liked to play it coy by keeping a brother waiting 'til at least the third ring."

Surry said, "When a man stands me up twice in the same month, I tend to want to know why, so I answered your call quickly. No games, I just want answers."

He heard the twinge of anger in her voice and figured she had reason to be angry. He should have called earlier to tell her about how crazy things had gotten after she left. Now, instead of her trying to make things up to him, it was his turn. "Baby, I promise this wasn't done on purpose. My client's schedule blew up in our faces and we had to spend hours putting it back together." He hesitated, but when she didn't say anything, he added, "I'm still a little hungry, so if you want to go to dinner now, I can swing by and pick you up."

"No, don't worry about it. I fixed a salad and a sandwich about an hour ago, so I'm good."

"What about tomorrow night?" he offered. "Anything you want to do. Just name it and I'm yours."

"Ian, do you really think I'm that insensitive? I know you have tons of work to do to get Juan's campaign up and running. Also, I'm really busy right now. I sign the contract with Roukes tomorrow and then I have to work out some details with my father on the new boutique we'll be opening in Dallas."

"I'm glad that worked out for you," Ian said.

"Thanks to you," Surry acknowledged. "I am so grateful to you for whatever you did to get John Michael to tell the truth. If you hadn't helped me, I wouldn't be signing this contract tomorrow."

"It was nothing," he said modestly.

"No, Ian. It meant everything to me, and if you hadn't been so upset with your father when you came to my hotel room last week, I would have told you that."

Hearing Surry say that his help meant everything

to her warmed his heart. He would do anything for this woman, whether she thanked him or not. But those words felt so good coming out of her mouth. He didn't want to harp on it and take the chance of scaring her away from him. He knew that Surry didn't like needing anyone, so he said, "It sounds like you're going to be busy this week, too."

"I am."

"Then what shall we do?" Ian hated to admit it, but Surry was right about the amount of work he had waiting on him. And he knew she had a business to run also. But he still wanted to see her.

"We're going to work hard, so we'll have some money when we play hard."

"Surry, you are something else. Any other woman would be biting my head off right now, but you seem cool about the whole thing."

"You called to let me know what's going on, so I'm good."

Ian pulled into the driveway of his home and turned off the ignition as he told her, "But I still want to take you out tomorrow night. You name it. Just tell me where you want to go."

Surry laughed. "I know you, Ian. You're a workaholic, just like me. You just got this client. So you'll need a few days to put your plan in motion. So, why don't you just get your work done this week and then you can go to Dallas with me this weekend."

"Do you think you'll have time for me this weekend? Sounds like you have a lot of business to handle."

"I'm also going to be with family. My mother wants me to come for dinner."

"Your parents, huh?"

"Yeah, are you okay with that?"

"This must be serious if you want me to meet your parents."

"More than you know, Ian. So, don't wuss out on me. I want to show you off."

Smiling at the thought of Surry wanting to show him off to her family, Ian said, "All right. It's a date. Can we leave early Saturday morning?"

"That works for me."

Ian wanted to see Surry so bad, he was prepared to turn his car around and drive all the way to the other side of town at this moment. He said, "You know, I could just drive over there tonight."

"You just left the office and you have an entire campaign to build, so I know you're tired, Ian. Just go home and go to bed."

She was right again. He needed the rest. "So, I'll see you in a few days."

Ian was about to hang up when Surry said, "You're not off the hook from calling me this week, though. I still want to hear your voice."

He'd talk to Surry all day long if he didn't have a business to run. He didn't know how she managed it, but this woman had his heart, and he didn't want to get it back. "You'll be the first person I talk to in the morning and the last person I speak to at night. Can you handle that?"

"Sounds good to me," Surry declared.

As they hung up, Ian drove into his garage, got out of his car and walked into his three-thousand-square-foot home. As he walked through the house that used to put a smile on his face every time he came home, because he bought it with his own money and didn't have to ask his family for anything, he now felt as if he had too much space for just one person. He put his hands on the sides of his mouth and yelled, "Hello."

No one answered. All he could hear was a slight echo. "Welcome home," he said to himself as he made a turkey sandwich, sat down at his kitchen table alone and ate it. Then he jumped in the shower and got into his king-size bed alone.

Chapter 15

Ian had been a man of his word. For the rest of the week, Surry had spoken to him first thing in the morning and late into the night. They were now on their way to Dallas to meet with her father and then have dinner with both her parents. Surry had the seat reclined a bit on the passenger side as Ian drove.

Now she knew what having a partner felt like. She didn't have to be Wonder Woman and do everything on her own. She was relaxing on the passenger side of the car, allowing her man to drive her where she needed to be, and loving it. Surry ran her hand up his arm and said, "Thanks for hanging out with me today."

"I wouldn't be anywhere else."

"With all the craziness we've been going through, I also forgot to ask about something that's been on my mind."

"And that is?" Ian asked, keeping his eyes on the road.

"How did you get John Michael to leave me alone?"

Smiling, he asked, "Are you still worried that I might have roughed him up?"

Shaking her head, Surry told him, "No, I believe that you know people who know things, and I want to know what you found out."

"You got that right." Ian took his eyes off the road long enough to wink at Surry.

Okay, she had sufficiently stroked his ego. He was the king of the jungle. The most powerful man on earth...yadda, yadda, yadda. "Tell me, already. What did you do?"

"It wasn't sexy or anything. Let's just say John Michael has an interesting way of counting dependents."

"Huh?"

Explaining himself, he said, "John Michael apparently thinks it's okay to claim his nieces and nephews on his tax returns, even though they don't live with him."

"It figures that someone accusing others of stealing would be a crook himself."

"Isn't that always the way it works?" Ian agreed.

They kept talking the entire four hours of the ride. Conversation was easy for them as they laughed, poked fun at each other and generally just enjoyed the trip so much that they made a four-hour drive in what felt like two.

When they reached her father's dress shop, she got out of the car, stretched her arms and legs and then pointed across the street. "If you're hungry, there's a sub shop right across the street."

"I can wait until we get to your parents' house. I don't want to offend your mother by being too full to eat her food."

Surry almost told Ian that his very presence would offend her mother, who lived to be unhappy. But she didn't want to scare him off. "Okay, but don't blame me if you pass out before we get there."

"Pass out?" Ian said incredulously as he beat on his chest. "I've never passed out in my life. Are you kidding?"

"Okay, my superhero. I'll never forget that. No passing out for Ian Duncan." She looped her hand around his arm and walked with him toward her father's dress shop. Just like last week, the dress shop had quite a few paying customers. Her father was doing just fine, and once they finalized their partnership, Surry was confident that he'd be doing even better.

Willy came toward them as they walked in the door. "You're early," he said as he hugged Surry.

Surry pointed at Ian and said, "He drives like a maniac." Her father looked at Ian, and then Surry said,

"Dad, this is Ian Duncan. He and I are..." She looked at Ian for clarification as to what they were doing.

Ian said, "Dating," as he put one arm around Surry and stuck his free hand out to her father.

"Ian, this is my Dad, Willy McDaniel."

Ian and Willy shook hands. "Nice to meet you, Mr. McDaniel."

"Oh, call me Willy."

Surry reached into her oversize handbag and pulled out a folder. "My attorney looked over the financial information you sent over and now I have the contract. You might want to have your attorney review it before signing. But once that's finished, we will be partners."

They hugged again and then Willy took the folder from her.

"We see that you're busy, so we won't hang around here. I'll take Ian to the house so he can meet Mom."

A look that Surry couldn't decipher flashed across her father's face and then he said, "I have extra help in the store today, so give me a moment to grab my keys and I'll head home with you right now."

Surry and Ian waited for her father to get his keys and then they followed him to the house. Sylvia was waiting for them. She kissed Surry and Ian on the cheek and then backed up and took a good look at Ian.

"Not bad, Surry. I can see why you've gone gaga over this man," Sylvia said.

"And if you don't mind my saying," Ian began,

"I can see why Willy went gaga for you, Mrs. McDaniel."

Her man was a charmer, and Surry appreciated Ian saying that because her mother was an exotic beauty whom her father had fallen for the moment they met. She had always loved her mother and looked to her wisdom to help guide the way she led her life. But lately, Surry had been wondering about a few things. For one thing, it bothered Surry that her mother complained about her father and his business and acted as if they were two seconds away from a going-out-of-business sale. But after her accountant reviewed the financial records of her father's business, Surry had gotten her answer. Willy McDaniel wasn't going to be a millionaire with his current business, but he was making a comfortable living. Her mother was obviously one of those women who could never be satisfied, and she prayed that she would never become that.

They sat down in the family room while her mother put the food on the table. Once she had gotten everything set, she asked them to join her in the dining room. "Ian, you can take the chair next to me and Surry can sit next to her father," Sylvia told the group.

Everyone sat down and began passing around plates of asparagus, wild rice, salmon, and lemon and dill sauce to go on top of the fish.

"The food looks wonderful, Mrs. McDaniel," Ian said as he filled his plate.

"Thank you, Ian. I hope you like it," Sylvia said as she scooped some rice onto her plate.

Surry noticed that her mother hadn't invited Ian to call her by her first name as her dad had. She hoped that Ian hadn't noticed the slight or if he had, she hoped he wouldn't be bothered by it. Her father had always been friendlier than her mother. That's just the way things were in the McDaniel household.

"So, Ian, Surry tells me that you are fabulously successful. Would you mind telling me what this career of yours is all about?" Sylvia took a bite of her fish, but kept her eyes glued on Ian.

"Mother! Don't drill him on his first visit," Surry said.

"Sorry," Sylvia raised her hands. "This is the first man you've brought home, so I don't really know the rules."

"I don't mind telling you what I do," Ian said as he put his fork down. "I work in politics. But I'm not a politician."

"How long have you been in politics? And what kind of work do you do, since you're not a politician?" Sylvia asked.

"I've been in politics since I was nineteen. I am a campaign manager when needed and a political analyst when not."

"And are you needed right now, or are you just trying to make yourself useful?" She was relentless in her questions.

"Sylvia, that's none of our business. Just let the man enjoy his meal and leave him alone," Willy said as he shook his head.

"Ian is very much in demand," Surry told her mother.

Ian glanced over at Surry and then turned back to her mother. "I am working for one of our state senators right now. He is seeking the mayor's office."

"Mayor." Sylvia said the word with a curled lip. "That's pretty small potatoes for someone who's been in business for over a decade." She pointed at him. "You must be at least thirty."

"I'm thirty-one."

"Old enough to have made a success of yourself by now. So, what's your holdup? When will you find success?" Sylvia pointed toward Willy. "Or are you like my husband over there? Do you plan to wait for a child of yours to grow up and show you how to make your way successfully?"

"That's enough, Sylvia. You can hold me in contempt all you want, but I will not sit by and allow you to do this to a friend of Surry's." His fist slammed against the table. "Enough is enough already."

But Surry couldn't let it go. She expected this dinner to go well. Ian was the man of her dreams, but her mother was trying to make him look as if he had nothing going for himself, the same way she had convinced Surry that every other man she'd dated had nothing going for him. But Surry knew better this time. Since Ian wasn't opening his mouth to defend himself, she decided to do it for him. "Ian has a great career, Mother. He's had his choice to work with governors, senators and even a presidential campaign. He chose to work with Juan Manuel because he believes that Juan has a future in politics."

Sylvia turned to Ian, astonishment in her eyes. "You chose a mayor over a president?" When he didn't respond, she turned back to Surry and asked, "Is he crazy or just stupid?"

The ride home was not as peaceful as the morning ride had been. Ian was furious that Surry felt the need to defend his career choices to her god-awful mother. He knew in his gut that Surry was the one. She was the woman he wanted to wake up to every morning, but if she didn't believe in him…there was no way he was going to allow her to make him miserable for the rest of his life.

"Okay, spill it. You've been surly this whole ride. So, just tell me what's wrong before you run off and leave me the same way I did you."

His hands tightly gripped the steering wheel. "And you think I'd do that?"

Surry put her hand on Ian's arm. "What's wrong, babe? Don't shut me out. I really want this to work."

What he really didn't understand was how Surry didn't already know what was wrong with him. "Weren't you at the same table with me?"

She ran her hand up and down his arm. "I know my mother can be a little hard to take."

"A little hard to take," he mimicked. "The woman acted as if I was some layabout with no direction in life." After saying that, Ian's thoughts drifted to the day Surry came to his office and confessed that she'd run away from him and the new relationship they'd been building because she was afraid that he had no direction. Now he knew where those worries came from. The woman must drive her husband absolutely crazy with her inability to understand that the journey is what makes success so sweet.

"She wasn't that bad, Ian."

"Were you in the same room? And did you see the look on your father's face? That man has been dealing with your mother's crap for so long that she's beat him down with it."

"I will give you that. Recently, I have noticed that she doesn't seem to be happy with anything my dad does, even when he seems to be making a go of his store. I don't know why she's like that. I just hope she opens her eyes so she can see just how great my dad is." She looked out the window and watched a car go by as she added, "I've discovered how wonderful my father is, and I'm not going to let my mother say another word against him to me ever again."

"Look, Surry, I know we're discussing your mom, so I'm really trying not to say everything I want to say. But what you must know is that even though I don't like the way she talked to me, what bothered me the most was the way you told your mom that I had my choice between other clients and the one I had, as if any of those other clients were better than the one I have now."

"I was just trying to stand up for you...like a girlfriend should. You did tell my dad that we were dating, remember?"

If he wasn't driving, he would have turned to her and looked her in the eye as he said what he had to say. But he couldn't take his eyes off the road if he wanted them to get home safely. "Surry," he began with a sigh, "I don't just want to date you. I want us to be together for a long time to come. But I don't want my woman feeling as if she has to make excuses for the career choices that I make."

"I wasn't making excuses. I was simply letting my mother know how in demand you are."

Ian didn't know how to make Surry see that she was acting like her mother by not acknowledging that what he was doing was good enough. And if he couldn't get her to see that, Ian just wasn't sure if they could move forward.

Later that night when Surry was at home and preparing to get in bed, she replayed the conversation with Ian in her head again. She knew he was upset, but she wasn't quite getting what the big deal was. But she did know that her mother played a huge part in what had gone wrong tonight. Surry had let her mother come between the relationship she should've had with her father all these years. Sylvia had also run off every other man Surry dated. But this time was different, because this time Surry was in love.

She had no problem admitting that fact to herself. And she had no problem admitting that it would hurt worse than anything she'd experienced thus far in life if she lost Ian, so she simply refused to lose. Her mother was not going to ruin this one for her. She just needed to get Ian focused on progressing in his career, and then Sylvia McDaniel wouldn't have anything to complain about.

Surry knew just what Ian needed, and she would move heaven and earth if that's what it took to get him where he needed to be.

Chapter 16

Tuesday afternoon, Surry drove to the Houston airport and picked up Walter Duncan. She had contacted him the day before and told him that Ian needed him. Surry was surprised at how fast Ian's father booked a flight from California to Houston to come and see about his son. That in itself showed Surry how much Walter cared about Ian. Now all she had to do was convince Ian of his father's love and then all would be as it should be…she hoped.

"Thank you for coming so quickly, Walter. I can see that you really care about your son," Surry told him as she opened her trunk so he could put his bag in.

"Of course I care about Ian," Walter proclaimed.

"I just don't know how to convince that stubborn son of mine that I care. Trouble is, he's just too much like his old man."

"That's why I'm here. I believe I'll be able to help," Surry told him as they drove off from the airport.

"Surry is an unusual name. What does it mean?"

"Surry is short for Sojourner. My mom named me after Sojourner Truth." Surry said those words with pride. As a young child, Surry understood the weight of carrying such a powerful name.

"So my son has got himself a self-made woman, capable of doing anything a man can, and do it better." Walter looked at her with respect in his eyes.

"What do you mean?" Who had been talking to this man about her?

"You know…the famous speech given by Sojourner Truth. I think it was titled 'Ain't I a Woman.'"

Her eyes bugged. "You know that speech?"

"I'm a student of history," Walter said.

Surry was impressed. Sojourner had indeed declared that she could do anything just as well as any man. Surry had lived her life that way—that is, until she met Ian. He had a way about him that allowed her to be okay with working with him, rather than trying to prove that she could do the work without him. She told Walter honestly, "The words of that speech used to be my mantra. But Ian showed me that it's okay to have a partner you can lean on from time to time."

"I'm glad you and my son are doing so well. He deserves some happiness."

Surry heard the wishful tone in Walter's voice, as if he himself was still waiting to have his own happiness. And Surry got the distinct impression that this man would not be happy until he and his son mended the rift between them. Ian was hurting also. She knew that he hadn't wanted to let go of a client like Governor Monroe. She just hoped that after Ian and his father cleared things up that the job was still available for him.

"Does Ian know that I am here?" Walter asked, a bit nervous.

"No, he's still too stubborn to know what's good for him," she said as she continued driving to Ian's office. "I told him I was bringing a picnic lunch. But he thinks the lunch is for me and him."

"Do you think this is wise? I wouldn't want you to do anything that would pull you and Ian apart."

Surry didn't know how wise this decision was, but she wanted her man to succeed in everything his hands touched. To do that, he needed this relationship with his father, whether he knew it or not. "Maybe he will thank me, you never know," Surry said as she pulled into the parking lot. Walter had a doubtful expression on his face, but she ignored it.

"We're here." She parked the car and got out.

Walter also exited the car.

Surry opened her trunk and took the picnic basket

out. She then handed Walter his bag and they entered the office building.

Walter stood back, looking around. He nodded his approval and then caught up with Surry. "How much space does Ian have in this building?"

"He has the first and second floor. The other sixteen floors are occupied by other businesses." She pointed to the reception area where she had patiently waited for Ian on a few occasions. "Have a seat right there and I'll come and get you."

"Okay," Walter said as he sat down.

Janice, Ian's secretary, saw Surry coming and said, "He's waiting for you. Go on in."

"Thanks, Janice." Over the past few weeks Surry had gotten to know Janice and liked the woman. She knocked once on Ian's door and then opened it. "Hey, handsome," she said as she walked in and put the picnic basket on his desk.

"Hey, your beautiful self," he said as he stood up and kissed her.

She loved kissing this man. He was everything she ever wanted, and his lips felt so good connected with hers. When the kiss was over, she said, "That was a nice welcome."

"I've got more where that came from."

She held up a hand, pushing him backward. "Calm yourself down. We have a few things to get out of the way before you have to get back to work."

"And why are you playing hooky today? I know you have tons of work to do yourself."

She opened her basket and took out a deli-made sandwich and soup and set them in front of Ian. "I don't mind taking a little time off to come see about my man."

"Watch it, now. Don't get me used to something that you won't be able to keep on doing." Ian sat back down and pulled his food closer to him.

She pulled the other sandwich and soup out of the basket as she told him, "I'm not about to spoil you and get you all babyish to the point you start getting on my nerves. This is a special occasion. So, don't get used to this."

He opened his soup, saw that it was creamy potato, licked his lips and then asked, "What's the special occasion? Are you one of those women who want to commemorate every month's anniversary?"

She gave him a strange look and then realized that they had indeed been dating for a month. She thought it was so sweet that he had remembered. But she wasn't about to celebrate each month. For one thing, the realization that they had been dating only a month didn't track well with the way her heart felt. How was she to know that when she finally fell that it would be so hard and so fast? "No, Ian, we have something else to celebrate."

He didn't say anything. He just looked at her, waiting for the answer.

She grabbed his hands and held them. "I know that you might be a little upset with me about this, but I want you to know that I did it for your own good."

"You're sounding like my mother telling me to eat my peas."

She couldn't hold it off any longer. "I picked your father up from the airport today." The look on her face held excitement.

The look on Ian's face was pure horror.

"Ian, come on. It's not that bad. Walter really cares about you and he wants to talk with you so the two of you can hash out your differences."

Ian stood up and walked over to the window in his office, needing space. In a low, controlled voice, he asked, "Why did you do this?"

"I'm trying to help you, Ian. If you would stop being so stubborn you'd realize that."

He put his hands in his pockets and turned to face her. "What exactly do you think I need help with?"

"Well...with getting Governor Monroe back as a client." She walked over to him. "I know how happy you were when you had the opportunity to work on a presidential campaign. Your father can get that back for you. All you have to do is forgive him so the two of you can move forward."

He stared at her for a moment, shook his head and then said, "You don't know me at all, do you?"

"Of course I know you, Ian. And I know what you

want out of your career. I'm just trying to help you get it, like you helped me."

"This is nothing like what I did. You asked for my help. I never asked you to get involved in this issue I have with my dad." His hands came out of his pockets and he began angrily waving them around as he shouted at her.

"Lower your voice, Ian. Your father and Janice are out there." She bobbed her head toward his door.

"Don't tell me to lower my voice. I don't care who's out there. I want to know why you did this."

She shot a glance at the door and whispered, "I already told you why I asked him to come here."

"But I already have a client. So I don't need my father for that."

"But you don't have the one that you really want." Surry wanted to jump up and down, scream at Ian… anything to get him to see reason.

"That's not true," Ian declared. "I don't have the client you and your mother want me to have. But I am happy representing Juan. But I'd like to know why you are not okay with the work I'm doing." He sat down on his couch and gave her the floor.

"You're only representing Juan because you passed on Governor Monroe. You told me yourself that you want to be a kingmaker. Stop looking a gift horse in the mouth and just take the job, Ian. I really think you're going to regret sulking like some little boy and accepting this mayor campaign when you could be so much more."

He pointed an accusing finger at her as he stood back up and got in her face. "There it is right there." He closed his eyes and took a deep breath, gaining control of himself as he added, "I knew that your mother had a lot of influence on you, but stupid me, I convinced myself that you weren't like her. But you are just like that woman."

"What are you talking about, Ian? I'm just trying to help you."

He paced around the room, hands flailing as he talked. "Yeah, I'm sure your mother tried to help your dad a whole bunch, too. Only trouble is, I don't want this kind of help."

"Why are you so angry?" Tears were forming in Surry's eyes. She knew Ian would be miffed because she went behind his back, but she hadn't imagined that he'd become so angry that he would speak to her the way he was at this moment. She flopped down on the couch, distraught, not knowing what to do to make this right.

"I'm angry because you don't believe in me!" he shouted.

She got in his face. "I do believe in you, idiot. I'm in love with you!" Tears were flowing down her face, but it didn't matter. He was pushing her buttons and she was mad and ready for a fight.

Ian rubbed his temple with his fingers. "Go home, Surry."

"What?" Did he just dismiss her? "Did you hear what I just told you?"

"I heard you. But it's not going to work." He strode toward his door and grabbed the handle. "I want you to leave."

"You don't mean that, Ian. Don't do this." Surry hated the sound of her voice as she watched the man whom she had fallen in love with turn into someone she didn't even recognize. But one thing was for sure—he no longer wanted to be bothered with her, and she wasn't going to keep begging him to listen to reason. Surry stood up.

The door burst open and Walter stepped in. He looked toward Ian and reprimanded him. "Why are you in here shouting at Surry? She doesn't deserve to be treated this way by you."

"This isn't your business, Dad. This is between me and Surry," Ian said defiantly.

"It's not between us anymore. I know when I'm not wanted. So, I'm going to do as you suggested and get out of here." She stalked by Ian and his dad without a backward glance. No one had ever spoken to her in such a manner, and she wasn't going to put up with it from Ian. She didn't care how much her heart was breaking right now. She was just going to have to get over it.

"Your turn, Dad. You might as well follow Surry so you don't miss your ride."

"I'm not going anywhere until you and I get a few things straight."

"Like what?"

"Your bad attitude doesn't scare me, son."

"Why should it? I doubt if there is much that could scare any man who could turn his back on his own son."

Walter closed Ian's door. He grabbed the sandwich and bowl of soup that Surry had left on Ian's desk and took a seat on the sofa. "Surry went through a lot of trouble to get us this food, so we might as well eat it."

"She picked it up from a deli. It's not like she cooked the soup from scratch."

Walter ate a few spoonfuls of his soup and then opened his sandwich. "I don't care where she got it from. This soup is delicious."

His father obviously wasn't leaving, and Ian was hungry. So, he grabbed his food off the desk and sat down in the chair next to his sofa and began eating, as well. Neither of them spoke for a while. They were too busy fueling up for the fight to come.

But once they finished eating, Ian's dad surprised him by finally being honest.

Walter said, "You were right, son. I did have something to do with you getting the assignment with Monroe."

"I knew it," Ian quickly said.

Walter held up a hand. "But not for the reasons you think." Walter leaned forward, imploring his son to listen. "I'm not interested in being known as some maker of kingmakers as you think."

Ian walked over to his desk, looked in Surry's basket and pulled out two cans of soda. He handed one to his dad and popped open the other. "Why'd you do it, then?"

"Because I recognize talent when I see it. What you've been doing with the campaigns you handled over the years is better than anything I've done throughout my entire career."

Ian was stunned that his father, the man who had thrown him off a campaign, was now complimenting him in a manner that Ian had never expected. "You've got three presidential elections to your credit. How can you possibly think I'm doing better than you?"

He stretched his arms wide and said, "Hey, I was lucky. But, you have real skill." His tone had been light, but now he turned serious. "I should have fired you, Ian. What you did was wrong, and it cost us that election."

Ian nodded. He couldn't do anything else but agree with that. If any of his staffers did what he'd done back then, he would have fired them on the spot also. But it just hurt more when it came from his own father, a man he had greatly respected.

"What I'm trying to say is, although you should have been fired, I could have handled the entire situation better. I never should have said that you had no future in politics, because I was completely wrong."

Now tears were forming in Ian's eyes. All these years as he worked his way through one difficult situation after another, he'd wished he could call his father and ask for advice. But that door had been closed to him. If his father had called and apologized to him a few years ago, Ian would have been more receptive to it. But now… "So much time has passed, Dad. I just don't know how to process this."

"We're family, Ian. All I'm asking for is your forgiveness. Can you do that for me, son? Can you forgive your foolish old man?"

Ian was silent…trying to put everything he was hearing into perspective.

"I heard about Juan Manuel."

Ian perked up and looked at his father. He hadn't needed this man's approval since he was nineteen, but now that Surry had shown him that she didn't believe in him or his plans, he needed someone to tell him that he wasn't crazy. So he asked, "What do you think of him?"

"He's a winner, son. That one could go all the way."

And with that, something in Ian broke. He didn't want to be angry anymore. He wanted his dad back. It no longer mattered that this man tried to hinder his dreams. Ian rushed over to his father, wrapped his arms around him and, with tears flowing down his face, said, "I'm ready, Dad. I forgive you."

They hugged and cried together, and then they sat back down and began to catch up. Their relationship had been stilted for so long that they had to regain their comfort level. But once they did, it was like old times.

After a while, Walter asked Ian, “So, what are we going to do about getting your woman back?”

Chapter 17

"Why don't you make these outfits in numerous colors? Every time I come in here, I see a dress or a pantsuit that I absolutely love, but it's not in the color I'm looking for."

Why did everyone want her to change? To be who they wanted her to be? "What color are you looking for?" Surry asked. After being dismissed from Ian's office, Surry drove to her boutique and decided to work, hoping that would take her mind off her aching heart. But after two hours of dealing with customers and trying not to cry on their shoulders, Surry couldn't take it anymore.

The woman picked up a navy blue dress and said, "This would be absolutely divine in yellow."

"We don't have that dress in yellow."

The woman put her hands on her hips and demanded, "Aren't these your designs? Can't you just call your factory in China or wherever and tell them to make me one of these dresses in yellow?"

Surry exploded. "Have you lost your mind? No one is wearing yellow in the wintertime." She snatched the dress from her customer, put it back on the rack and then told the woman, "If you want to dress like a banana, go down the street to Felt's. They have all sorts of weird stuff in there."

Brenda Ann rushed over to Surry and, while the customer stood in shocked silence, pulled Surry aside. "What are you doing?"

"I was trying to help this lady," Surry announced as if she hadn't just been rude to the woman.

"I'll help her. Why don't you go to the break room for a minute?" Brenda Ann didn't wait for a response from her boss. She stepped over to the customer and began apologizing for Surry's actions.

At first Surry was offended. She was Brenda Ann's boss and could say whatever she wanted to these customers. But that was only if she didn't want to have very many customers, she quickly reminded herself. She went into her break room, sat down on the sofa and bawled her eyes out.

"What's wrong, Surry?" Brenda Ann asked as she stepped into the break room.

"I should have never come to work today. Thank you for helping with that customer."

"I gave her a twenty-percent-off coupon. I hope that was okay."

Wiping away the tears from her face, Surry agreed, "Yes, that was perfect. I just hope she'll come back."

"Can I do anything to help, Surry? I hate seeing you like this."

"Thanks, Brenda Ann." She stood up and grabbed her keys. "I just need to go home. Can you handle the store without me today?"

Brenda Ann nodded. "Just go get you some rest."

Surry got in her car and instantly thought about the brownies and ice cream Danetta used to eat when she and Marshall had problems. She needed that sweet treat so badly right now, but she didn't want to go in the store when she couldn't stop herself from crying.

She picked up her cell and called Danetta. When her friend picked up the phone, she said, "I know you're at work, but I was hoping that you could stop by my condo when you're done for the day."

"Let me check with Marshall and make sure that he didn't plan anything for us this evening."

"Okay," Surry said as the tears formed again, even though she tried so hard to hold them back. "Do me a favor, Danetta. If you can come, bring those brownies you used to get. Oh, and don't forget the ice cream," Surry said with a sniff.

"Oh, sweetie, are you crying?"

She sniffed again. "Yeah, but I don't want to talk about it right now, okay? I'd go pick up the brownies myself, but I don't want to show my face in a store today."

"I'm leaving work now. I'll meet you at your condo in about an hour," Danetta told her.

"But you have to work, and you haven't talked to Marshall yet."

"Girl, my man and I own this place. I can run out of here anytime I feel like it. And you need me, so Marshall won't mind if I can't spend the evening with him. Now, get yourself home. I can still hear you sniffling."

"I'm sorry. I'm just falling apart."

"I'll see you in a bit. Is it okay if I call Ryla?"

"Yes, I really don't want to be alone right now. So, please call her." Surry hung up, realizing that for the second time in the space of a month she had actually confessed to needing someone. If her namesake was looking down on her right now, what would the woman think? Surry was no Sojourner Truth, that was for sure. But she was Sojourner McDaniel, and she needed to learn her own special kind of truth.

She drove home rubbing her eyes and trying to remind herself of her mantra. She was a woman and she could do anything just as well as any man could… well, maybe almost anything, because she doubted she'd be able to fix her broken heart on her own. All these years she had avoided love because her mother convinced her that it wasn't worth it, that men only served to disappoint. And once she'd finally found a man she could give her heart to, he went and proved her mother right.

"That's not true," Danetta said when Surry expressed the same sentiment to her.

Brownies, ice cream, cherries, nuts, whipped cream and chocolate syrup were on the coffee table. Surry, Ryla and Danetta filled their bowls with the ooey-gooey goodness, and then the three of them sat on the floor in Surry's spacious living room.

Surry was in her pajamas and was prepared to eat her way into a bigger size by nightfall. "It is true, Danetta. Just look at how things turned out."

Ryla put her hand on Surry's shoulder. "Surry, this is not as bad as you think. I know Ian cares about you. He has said as much to Noel, and he has no reason to lie to a friend of his."

"You didn't see the way he looked at me today, the way he treated me." She was practically blubbering as tears ran down her face. "I never thought love was supposed to hurt like this."

"It does," Danetta confirmed. "I've been where you are." She held up her bowl of brownies topped with vanilla ice cream. "Whenever Marshall would start dating a new woman, instead of telling him how I felt about him and that I wanted us to build a life together, I would drown my sorrows in this." She took a bite and closed her eyes to savor it. "Oh, how I've missed this. I think being pregnant entitles me to a double helping." She got up and began filling her bowl again.

"You don't have to use pregnancy as your excuse. Just come over to my house from now on, because it seems like the sorrows have just begun over here." Surry scooped up a healthy heap of ice cream and plopped it into her mouth.

"Don't you remember how distraught I was when Noel left me on our honeymoon? I couldn't eat, think or do anything but sleep. But I pulled myself together and went and got my man back. And that's what I suggest you do also."

"No thank you, Mrs. Ryla Carter. You're the one who got me in the situation. If I hadn't listened to you about going to see Ian in the first place, I wouldn't be here like this right now."

"And you wouldn't be growing your business, nor would you have just signed that multimillion-dollar deal you just signed. Think about it..." Ryla stood up and swept her arms about dramatically. "Because of me, you can now go on that show *How I Made My Millions*." She pointed at Surry, warning her, "And I better hear my name mentioned as the friend who helped save your crumbling empire."

"I promise that I will tell the world about how Ryla Carter got me involved with a man who broke my heart."

Ryla collapsed back onto the floor. "I was trying to make you laugh, Surry. You are a wonderfully resourceful woman. Shouldn't we be able to sit here and come up with a solution to a heart problem, just as we come up with solutions for our businesses?"

What Ryla was saying sounded so reasonable and so simple. But Surry had learned that nothing was simple when the heart was involved. She had trusted in Ian, and he let her down. This was her reality, and no problem-solving technique was going to fix that, as far as Surry was concerned.

But oh, how she had loved being in that man's presence, kissing him, holding hands with him and just talking. Surry thought Ian Duncan was the man of her dreams, someone she could have children with and grow old with. All she'd wanted him to do was make peace with his father so that he could move forward in his career. But Ian had acted as if she'd spit in his face. "It will never work with me and Ian. He's too full of pride," Surry declared.

"Well, that makes two of you."

"How can you say that, Danetta? I have swallowed my pride in so many ways." When her friends didn't offer her an amen, she began ticking off the ways she had lost her pride. "I went to Ian and asked him for help. And, might I remind you that he refused to help me at first, but when he came back later offering his help, I didn't turn him down and declare I could handle everything on my own. I humbly accepted his offer."

Ryla giggled at that.

"What? Are you trying to say I wasn't humble about it?"

"Go on," Ryla told her friend. "Please continue enlightening us with your humble qualities."

"It's not funny, Ryla. I am humble. I've started attending church with you two, I'm nicer these days and I even begged Ian not to break up with me."

"Shut your mouth, girl. Now, you didn't tell us about that. Spill it. What happened?"

Surry hesitated for a moment. She'd needed her friends to get through this terrible day, but she hadn't wanted to confide everything, partly because she wondered if Ian had been right about her. And if he was right, then Surry felt as if she was doomed to a life of loneliness. She closed her eyes, silently prayed for strength and then trodded on. "I told you that Ian was angry because I called his father and then picked him up from the airport."

They nodded.

"But what I didn't tell you is that he said some awful things to me and even threw me out of his office."

"That doesn't sound like Ian," Ryla said with a puzzled look on her face.

"Oh, so now I'm a liar, too, huh?"

Danetta rubbed her friend's arm and consoled her. "Nobody thinks you're a liar, Surry. But Ian's actions do seem a bit off to us, so can you just tell us what he said to you?"

"He told me that I was just like my mother and that he wouldn't live the rest of his life with a woman like that."

"I do think that you worry too much about what your mother thinks, but you don't act like her," Danetta said and then asked, "Why does Ian think you act like her?"

Surry took a deep breath and then told everything. "He thinks that I don't believe in him. My mother had said that his taking on a mayor's race was like a demotion, so I thought that if he made amends with his dad that he might be able to get the campaign of his dreams back. The one where he was going to be working for a potential presidential candidate.

"But Ian is comfortable with the choice he made, and he doesn't want to be with me any longer because he thinks I will just keep putting his choices down, the way my mother does my dad *constantly.*" She said the word *constantly* as if the thought of what her mother did to her dad was draining on her.

When her friends didn't say anything, she looked up at them with fresh tears forming, as the truth of what she'd done began taking shape. "I messed up, didn't I? I let my mom get in my head again, and I blew it with Ian."

The three women hugged and cried together. Ryla and Danetta spent the next hour consoling Surry. But Surry could not be consoled, at least not yet. She dried her eyes and told her friends that they had to go home to their husbands.

"We can stay longer if you need us," Danetta assured.

"No." Surry shook her head. "I'll be fine. I'm getting a headache, so I just want to take a pain pill and go to sleep anyway."

"Okay, but I'll call you in the morning, and you better answer the phone or I'm going to come back over here and bust the door down," Ryla told her.

"I'll answer, I promise." She walked her friends to the door, and once they were out she picked up her telephone and called her mother, something she'd been itching to do since she figured out why she lost her man.

Sylvia answered on the second ring. "Well, hello," she said. "I was beginning to wonder if I even had a daughter since I hadn't heard from you since you left on Saturday. And by the way—" she trudged on "—don't bring that young man back with you if he's the reason you had to leave so suddenly. I expected you to spend the night."

"You don't have to worry about me bringing Ian back to your house, because he broke up with me."

"What?" Sylvia sounded astonished by this news. "How dare that second-rate loser of a campaign manager break up with you."

"That's just it, Mom. Ian is not second-rate. He's first-class all the way, but I allowed you to make me think that what he was doing wasn't good enough. And I leaped right in and messed up another relationship."

"You probably tried to help him and he took it the wrong way. Men are such idiots. You've got to lead them around by the hand or they won't do anything right."

Tears began forming in her eyes again, but this time they were for her mother—for all the joy in life that she must have missed because she simply refused to see anything other than the way she thought it should be. "Do you really believe that, Mother?"

"Yes," she declared. "If I didn't help your father, he'd probably be in a ditch somewhere."

Surry clenched her teeth in anger. "Daddy is doing just fine, Mother. But you've never been able to open your eyes and see what is right in front of you. Yeah, sure we had some hard times when I was growing up. But he kept at his business and it is now doing well."

"Your father should have accomplished this twenty years ago. We should be so much further along, but he can't seem to do anything right."

Surry was practically yelling at her mother now. "Not everyone can start a business with enough money in the bank to make everything happen at once. Success takes time. But you have never been able to give anyone the latitude they need to make things happen. You ran all of my boyfriends away. And now you've even ran away the man that I love.

"I don't know how I'm going to forgive you for this, Mother. I love you, so I'll be praying for the strength I need to forgive. But from this day forward, I need you to stay out of my head. No more talking Daddy down, or any man I choose to date for that matter."

"Where is all of this coming from?"

"It's coming from my broken heart, Mother. So, please, let me mend it and just leave me alone." When she hung up with her mother, she prayed harder than she'd ever prayed in her life. She needed to change, and with God's help, Surry had every confidence that her change was on the way.

Chapter 18

Sylvia had wanted nothing more in life than the little girl she'd given birth to almost thirty years ago. That Surry was upset with her was more than Sylvia could bear. It caused her to sit back and take a good look at herself. She didn't like what she saw. She hadn't started her marriage bitter. She'd been deliriously happy with Willy when they first married, but unpaid bills piled up, home repairs were neglected for lack of money and vacations were put off.

After a while she just began to see everything through a negative lens. Truth was, Willy had made progress in his business. And the rest of the truth was, the arthritis that claimed her hands had also claimed her career. She couldn't sew if she wanted to, and that fact had a lot to do with her unhappiness.

Sylvia knew her reasons for being so miserable and unhappy all the time, but she'd been like this so long, she didn't know if she could be any other way. But Surry still had a chance, and if it was the last thing she did on earth, Sylvia was going to fix her daughter's broken heart.

"Ian, what have you done to Surry?" Noel asked once he got his friend on the phone.

"We got into a big fight yesterday, and I'm still trying to figure out what I need to do about it."

"Ryla kept me up until about two this morning talking about how hurt Surry is and how she's never seen her like that. I've got to tell you that you're on Ryla's list, so I wouldn't show your face around here for a while."

"I just don't know what to do, man. I was really feeling Surry. I thought that she and I actually had a future, but after what she pulled..." He let the rest of his thoughts hang in the air because he was simply sick at heart and didn't want to tell another man that.

"Did you really throw her out of your office?" Noel asked.

"I asked her to leave."

"Man, I sure hope you know what you're doing, because Surry is sick over this. Ryla said that Surry has never been in love with anyone, but she's told them that she loves you."

"Let me talk to you later, Noel. I need to get back to all this work on my desk." Ian quickly hung up. He wasn't really working, because he couldn't concentrate. He just couldn't stand to hear that he had caused Surry so much pain. If things were different between them, he would run to her and try to make the situation better. But he couldn't run to a woman who thought that what he was doing with his life was small.

Yes, she had brought his father back into his life, and Ian was grateful for that. What he was having a hard time forgiving her for was the reason behind what she did.

His phone buzzed. It was Janice, his secretary. Ian was tempted to ignore her because he didn't feel like talking to anyone, but duty called. He punched a button on his phone. "What's up, Janice?"

"You have a visitor."

He glanced at his calendar. "I don't have anyone scheduled today. Did you put someone on my schedule and forget to tell me?"

"I wouldn't do that." Janice sounded offended as she added, "Her name is Sylvia McDaniel. She says that she is Surry's mother."

He took a deep breath and then blew it out. "Send her in. And hey, I'm sorry about my tone earlier. I didn't mean to accuse you of not doing your job."

"All is forgiven," Janice said brightly. "But if you could take a chill pill anytime soon, that would be helpful."

Everyone was making it their business to tell him how much of a Grinch he was. His dad had left town early that morning, but before he got out of Ian's car at the airport he made a point of telling him, "You shouldn't have spoken to Surry that way yesterday. I happen to like her. The two of you are a match."

Then Noel got on his case, and now even Janice was unhappy with him. Well, get in line, because he wasn't all that happy with himself, either. He'd lost Surry and he didn't see how he could ever get back with her, and the reason was getting ready to walk into his office now.

He stood up and walked around his desk, praying that he would be civil to this woman as she opened his door. "Mrs. McDaniel," he acknowledged.

"Ian, thanks for seeing me this morning." She walked over to him and put her hand out so they could shake, but the curve in her fingers made the action a bit awkward. "Forgive me," she said as she pulled her hand back and rubbed it. "This arthritis has made my life a living nightmare."

"Have a seat, Mrs. McDaniel." He pointed toward the sofa as he took a seat in the chair beside it. "What can I do for you?"

"You've got a really nice office building. Your office is spacious and you're in a good location," she said as her eyes darted around the room.

Ian wanted to say "Not so bad for a ne'er-do-well, huh?" but the gracious side of him would not allow that. He simply nodded and said, "Thank you. We like it."

She turned back to him, pursed her lips and then let out a frustrated sigh. "I came to see you today because I owe you an apology. You see, I'm a mom, so no man is ever good enough for my daughter as far as I'm concerned. But I had no idea how badly I was influencing Surry until she called me in tears yesterday."

Now he was feeling like the world's biggest jerk. How could he have hurt Surry so badly? She was in pain and he was at fault. His father was right. He never should have spoken to her the way he had.

"You see, my daughter has never really been serious about anyone she's dated before."

"She's never been serious about them because Surry knew that none of the men she dated would ever measure up to your standards."

Sylvia shook her head. "It was never my standards any of them had to worry about. Surry has her own standards, and evidently you more than meet her requirements. As a matter of fact, she told me that you were first-class all the way. And that she'll never meet another man as grand as you. She even told me to butt out of her business from now on."

Surry had said all of that to her mother? Ian was

floored. Because the reason he didn't think it could work for him and Surry was because he never imagined he'd be able to get her away from the stranglehold her mother appeared to have on her.

"You see, Ian, my daughter loves you. So, the question you need to answer for yourself is do you love her? And is your love for her strong enough that you'd even be willing to fight me for her?" With that, Sylvia stood. "I don't want to take up any more of your time. I'm sure you have much work to do with that new client of yours." She headed to the door, put her hand on the knob, opened it and then turned back to Ian. "Oh, and by the way, call me Sylvia. Mrs. McDaniel just seems so formal."

Surry had dried her eyes and washed her face, determined that she was going to meet this new day head-on. As the Bible says, "Weeping may endure for a night, but joy comes in the morning." It was time for Surry to embrace the joy that she had discovered after a long night of soul searching.

She loved her mother, and that would never change. Sylvia McDaniel had done so much for her over the years, and Surry couldn't discount that just because her mother had an awful disposition at times. But from this point on, Surry knew that the relationship with her mother had shifted. She no longer needed her approval, and that felt good and right.

She stood on the outside of her boutique. She

looked up at the building, loving what she had created. But today she was able to appreciate her success, with an understanding that this was not all she wanted out of life. After experiencing how good love with the right man could be, she decided that she wanted that, too. Her heart was hurting because of the way things ended between her and Ian, but she'd still choose to love again. She just had to wait for the right man to come into her life. And Surry promised herself that she wouldn't allow anything to stop her from loving the second time around.

She stepped into her store, noticing that several customers were already milling around. Brenda Ann rushed over to her, "Hey, Surry, how are you feeling?"

"I'm doing good." Surry was walking forward while Brenda was moving backward in front of Surry.

"Are you sure you're ready to come back to work today?"

Surry was thankful that she had Brenda. The woman knew her job and took pride in doing it right. She didn't even want Surry to damage the profits and image of her own boutique. Surry put her hands on Brenda Ann's shoulders. "I'm good. I cried my eyes out last night. I prayed about it, and now I'm here to work."

Brenda shrugged. "If you're good, then I'm good."

"Hey, I won't be the first woman to have to work while dealing with personal issues." She put a smile on her face and said, "Let's go make some sales."

And Surry meant every word she'd said. She wasn't going to let her problems with Ian interfere with her work…not today, anyway. "That color looks lovely next to your complexion," Surry said as she approached a customer.

The woman beamed. "Thanks, I think I'll buy it."

The day was going well. The store was racking up sales and Surry was enjoying the work. It took her mind off Ian and how badly things had turned out for them. Maybe if she didn't have such a need to fix every doggone little thing in life, she wouldn't have rushed to try to solve a problem that Ian hadn't wanted solved. But she wasn't going to dwell on it anymore. She was going to work through the rest of the day and then prepare herself for going home alone as usual.

At about one in the afternoon, the chime above the door jingled. She looked across the room to greet another customer and saw Ian walk through the door. This was not happening. She wasn't prepared to see this man. Not after the hateful things he'd said yesterday, not after how her heart broke so thoroughly through the night as she ached for one more chance with him. What if he was here to spew more venom at her? She wouldn't be able to take that, not while she was making her way through a fragile recovery.

She turned and tried to rush to her break room.

Ian held up a hand. "Wait, please don't leave."

Not wanting to look as if she couldn't handle herself with a mere man, she turned back around and said, "What do you want? Why are you in my place of business after you kicked me out of yours as if I was some loiterer?"

Brenda Ann was helping a customer. She turned around, spotted Ian and started nodding her head as if she had figured out what was wrong with her boss.

Other customers began looking their way as Ian said, "I'm here because I have a problem that only you can solve."

She crossed her arms and twisted her lip, displaying that he better bring it before she had him thrown out. Her thoughts were spiteful, but hey, her heart was involved.

"You see, there's this man who seems determined to ruin my life."

She dropped her hands instantly, as fear clenched her heart. She worried that John Michael had done something to hurt Ian in some way. The last thing she ever wanted was for Ian to be hurt after he had helped her retain her business. "What happened? Is it John Michael?"

"I wish it was. I'd have no trouble dealing with an enemy like that." He stepped closer to her, imploring her with his eyes. "The enemy I'm dealing with right now is much closer to me."

Now she was thinking that she'd made a terrible mistake all the way around by contacting Ian's dad. Maybe the man really didn't mean his own son any good. "Ian, I'm so sorry. You've got to believe me. I never thought your father would try to do anything against you."

He was in front of her now. He took her hand and pulled it to his heart. He shook his head. "It's not my dad, either. By the way, thanks for bringing him to town. We worked out most of our issues yesterday."

A tear sprung to her eye, for she was truly happy that Ian had found his way back to his father. She now had a relationship with her own father, and she was grateful for it. The two of them had wasted many years, holding anger for things that should have been forgiven long ago. However, Surry was learning that second chances were better than no chances at all.

"But," Ian added, "you need to know that I didn't ask for the Monroe campaign back. I believe that the campaign I have now is the one I should be focused on and that is good enough for me." He looked into her eyes, almost begging her to say the words he wanted to hear. "But I need to know that what I choose to do with my life is good enough for you."

Why did he even care what she thought? He had dismissed her. But maybe he needed this last thing from her so they could both go in peace. "Ian, you are already a success in my book. You are an intelligent, kindhearted man who goes after what he wants one hundred percent. So, I believe whatever you decide to do, you will be successful."

He took a deep breath and then plowed on. "The man I'm having trouble with is me, Surry. I said some things to the woman I love more than life itself, and I fear that she'll never forgive me...that she won't agree to spend the rest of her life with me."

"Oh, she can and she will," Brenda Ann said as the customers in the store began sending up hoots and shouts.

Ian dropped to one knee, took a three-carat diamond ring out of his jacket pocket and said, "What do you say, Surry? Will you marry me so we both will have someone to share our dreams with?"

Surry sucked in a breath and put her hand to her heart. She turned this way and that as she glanced at everyone in the store, gawking at this gorgeous man who had eyes only for her. This was her chance, and this time she wasn't letting anyone get in her way, not even herself.

"I forgive you, Ian, because that is what loving someone is all about. We take the good, bad and ugly and then roll it into one big bundle of love that we can hold on to, and grow and learn from."

Ian wiped a tear from his eye. That Surry could forgive him after his behavior yesterday was more than he deserved. He didn't take it lightly.

Surry stuck her hand out. "And yes, I will marry you."

Ian put the ring on Surry's finger, jumped up and pulled his woman into an embrace that was full of love, forgiveness and promises for the future.

Epilogue

Eight years later

Ian sat in a hotel room surrounded by staffers and Governor Juan Manuel. Everyone in the room was glued to the television as the election results rolled in. At ten fifty-six everyone in the room cheered when Ohio, that great swing state, was called for Juan. Ian hadn't cheered, though. It wasn't that he was pessimistic about the outcome. From the first day he signed on to work with Juan, he knew the man would one day become president of the United States.

Juan had served two years as mayor and four as governor, and he'd spent the past two years running for the top job. It was almost his, and Ian should be in the back room running the numbers with his staffers, but tonight his mind was on Surry.

They had been married for seven years—no children yet, but life was good for them. However, lately Surry hadn't been feeling well and he was worried.

Juan came over to him, put his hand on his shoulder and said, "Why don't you go see about her?"

Ian shook his head. "I promised that I would get you into the Oval Office, and I'm not leaving your side until my job is done."

"Your wife is in the room down the hall. It's not like you'd have to go far. Just check on her and come back. That way you'll have your head back in the game."

Ian had to admit that the governor was right. He couldn't do anything else for Juan tonight. All they were doing in this room was waiting for the results to come in, but Surry needed him now. He made his decision and got up and went down the hall to check on his wife. She'd been ill for the past few weeks of the campaign and was now throwing up. Ian had begged her to make a doctor's appointment. But she kept putting it off.

As he opened the door to their hotel room, Ian heard Surry scream and then start hollering, "Thank You, God. Thank You, thank You, God!"

Ian rushed into the room. When he didn't see her, he threw open the bathroom door. There she was, holding what looked like a pregnancy test. He pointed at it. “Is that what I think it is?”

She nodded fervently. “We did it, baby. I’m pregnant.”

Ian pulled his wife into his arms and kissed her forehead, her cheeks, her neck and then finally her mouth. They held on to each other as they had the day they married and imagined a life of love, laughter and lots and lots of kids.

They danced around the hotel room, celebrating their good news. The television was on, and Surry and Ian somehow heard the CNN announcer call California for Juan and then declare Juan the winner of the election.

“Baby, did you hear that?” Surry asked as her mouth dropped and she turned and pointed at the television.

“I heard it,” Ian said calmly.

“You know what this means, don’t you?” Surry asked, grinning from ear to ear. “I’m married to a kingmaker.”

Ian pulled her into his arms and said, “No, you married a baby maker, and that is truly the best of all.”

* * * * *

A new miniseries featuring fan-favorite authors!

The Hamiltons: Fashioned with Love

Family. Glamour. Passion.

Jacquelin Thomas

Styles of Seduction

Available September 2013

Pamela Yaye

Designed by Desire

Available October 2013

Farrah Rochon

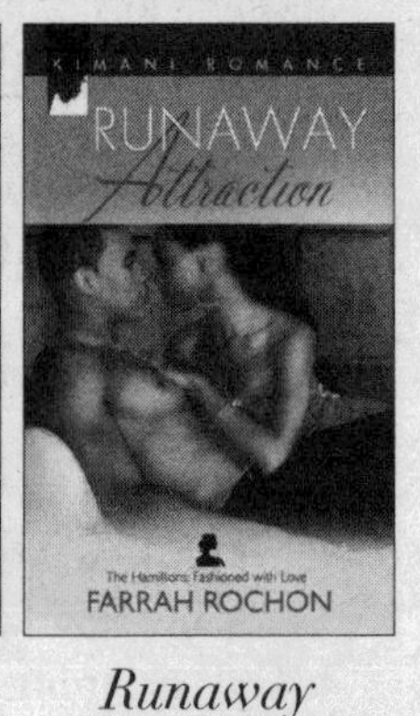

Runaway Attraction

Available November 2013

KPHFWLC13